D1046255

DIARY OF A SURFER VILLAGER

Books 1-5

(an unofficial Minecraft book)

By,
DR. BLOCK

Copyright © 2015-2019 by Dr. Block and DrBlockBooks.com; published by Lake George Press, a subdivision of Eclectic Esquire Media, LLC

ISBN: 978-1-7336959-2-3

No part of this publication may be reproduced, distributed, or transmitted in any form or by any means, without the prior written permission of the publisher, except in the case of brief quotations embodied in critical reviews and certain other noncommercial uses permitted by copyright law. **This unofficial Minecraft autobiography is an original work of fan fiction which is neither sanctioned nor approved by the makers of Minecraft. Minecraft is a registered trademark of, and owned by, Mojang AB, and its respective owners, which do not sponsor, authorize, or endorse this book.** All characters, names, places, and other aspects of the game described herein are trademarked and owned by their respective owners.

If you like this book, **please leave a review at your favorite online bookstore or book review site** so other Minecrafters can learn about it.

Thank you!

Table of Contents

BOOK 2

BOOK 3

DIARY OF A SURFER VILLAGER

Book 1

(an unofficial Minecraft book)

Day 1 – Lunchtime

So, it seems like all of my friends are keeping diaries these days. It is the latest rage among us villager kids.

So, I am going to keep my own diary too. I would not want to be left out.

The librarian in town has been selling blank diaries for only two emeralds.

So, I decided to buy a diary with my allowance.

Here it goes...

My name is Jimmy Slade, and I am a twelve-year-old villager. This is what I look like:

I live in a village called Zombie Bane. Cool name for a village, right?

The story behind the name goes like this: About two hundred years ago one of my ancestors – my great-great grandfather, Cornelius – single-handedly killed ten zombies in one night.

To honor this amazing feat, the villagers renamed the village. Since no one was going to name the village something as silly as "Cornelius Town," they named it "Zombie Bane" instead.

The killing of ten zombies by a single villager was and still is considered weird and amazing by villagers throughout the Overworld.

In fact, we get thousands of zombie-obsessed tourists every year who come to our village to see the exact locations where the zombies were killed.

They can even participate in the famous "Dead Zombie Scavenger Hunt."

For the low-low price of only ten emeralds [*wink* – total rip-off], a tourist gets a map showing the location where each zombie was killed by my great-great-gramps.

The tourist can go to that location and get a souvenir bobble-head zombie with a number on it: "1" for the first zombie killed, "2" for the second killed, etc. (Each bobble-head costs a mere four emeralds.)

At each location, tourists can buy all sorts of other things, like history books retelling the story of the zombie slaughter, souvenir robes that say "I slayed at Zombie Bane" on them, and of course, food and drinks.

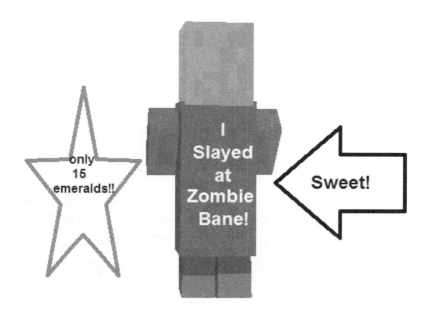

Why have we been able to make such a valuable industry out of this one event?

Because villagers are usually wimps who just run and hide from zombies whenever they see them. Of course, zombies normally only come out at night, so villagers can still move around during the day time.

So, all these tourist villagers come here to feel good about themselves. They like to think that maybe, under the right circumstances, they would be able to kill ten zombies all by themselves.

Of course, they are wrong because villagers only really care about money. Well, most villagers, anyway.

All of this tourist-industry action amuses me because, even though our village is called "Zombie Bane," I don't think any villager in my village has killed even one zombie in like 100 years or something.

They should change the name of our village to Zombie Lame.

I told my mom my idea about changing the village's name. She said that I was dishonoring the memory of my great-great-gramps.

I told her that I thought it was cool and all that he dominated on those ten zombies, and, like, I fully respect him for that, but that was like 200 years ago. Why did people still care?

She told me that people care about amazing things. People want to believe in something greater than themselves. They want to live their lives through the lives of others who do great deeds.

This did not make any sense to me. Why would someone want to pretend to live someone else's life?

And then she added, "Plus, because of your great-great-gramps, *may Notch rest his soul*, the entire village is more wealthy than any other village in all the world. The money we make from the tourist industry is amazing."

*** Drum roll, please! ***

And, there it is folks. What really motivates villagers: emeralds.

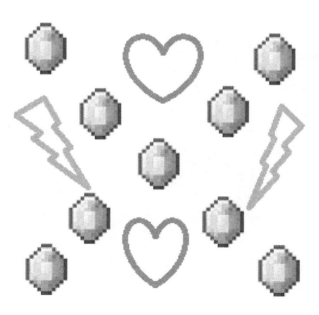

"You are just greedy like the rest of them, Mom," I said, shaking my head.

"What?" she said. "Do you want to toil in the fields all day growing watermelons to trade?"

I shrugged. "Maybe."

My mom laughed. "No, you don't. You want to sit in a store and sell cheap souvenirs to tourists."

I did not respond.

We sat in silence at the kitchen table. I was eating a pork chop, and my mom was counting a huge pile of emeralds.

Finally, she looked at me, holding a few emeralds in her hands, and said, "What *do* you want to do when you grow up, Jimmy?"

"I want to be a surfer," I said.

As my mom fainted, the emeralds she was holding clattered to the floor.

Day 1 – Evening

When my mom passed out, I ran next door and got the old lady who used to babysit me when I was a ... well ... a baby. She would know what to do.

I helped the old lady lift my mom onto a couch in the living room. The old lady put a cool, wet cloth on my mom's forehead.

"Your mother needs to rest," said the old lady. "When she wakes up, make her drink this."

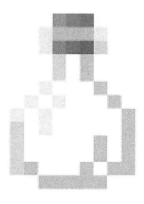

The old lady handed me some sort of potion. I think it was a potion of healing, but I really had no idea.

I nodded. "The whole thing?"

"Yes. She should be fine in no time."

"Okay, thank you."

As the old lady was getting ready to leave, she asked, "What happened to make your mom faint?"

I shrugged. "I'm not sure. I just told her I wanted to be a surfer, and then she passed out."

I watched as the old lady's eyes began to roll up into her head and she began to sway. *Was she going to pass out too?*

No, she was able to put a hand out and steady herself against a wall.

"No wonder she fainted," the old lady panted. "You can't be a surfer."

"Why not?"

"Because surfers are just no good lazy slobs who sit around at the beach all day," explained the old lady in her know-it-all voice.

"How do you know?" I asked. "Have you ever met a surfer?"

"No," she admitted. "But I've heard all about them. Useless."

"Whatever," I said, opening the door to my house to let her out. "Thanks for the potion."

The old lady did not like being dismissed by a twelve-year-old, but she had dismissed my dream and I was done talking to her.

After the old lady left, I sat in the living room chair near my mom, who was still unconscious on the couch.

As I sat there, I flipped through a copy of a surf magazine a player had traded to me for 5 emeralds a few months ago. It was the best trade I had ever made. It is why I want to be a surfer.

I looked at the pictures of the waves. They were rising out of crystal clear blue water in some tropical biome.

The surfers were turning their boards in radical ways, creating angles I had never seen. They weren't exactly square. I did not even have words to describe the turns.

The names of the places in the pictures were like poetry: Pipeline, Waimea, Teahupoo, Kirra, Lowers, Malibu, Mundaka, Supertubos, Cloudbreak.

Other pictures showed surfers *inside* the tube of the wave. It looked so peaceful. And then, the pictures of them being spat out of the tube. It must be what it is like to be born.

And the words they used to describe riding inside the tube were also amazing: in the green room, pitted, shacked, slotted, tubed, barreled, piped .... It felt like a magical and mysterious language.

I needed to do this.

I needed to go to these places.

I needed to be a surfer.

After a few hours, my mom finally woke up, and I gave her the potion. I could tell it worked quickly as her eyes brightened and she sat up on the couch.

Uh, oh, here it comes, I thought.

"Jimmy, you can't be a surfer," she said.

"Why not?" I asked, crossing my arms.

"Because you can't earn any emeralds doing it."

"There is more to life than emeralds, Mom."

My mom's mouth hung open in shock, like I had just told her that I was going to have a sleep over at Herobrine's house.

"Emeralds *are* life, son," she said. "If your father and I have taught you one thing, it is that nothing in life matters more than emeralds."

"What about the dreams of your only child?" I asked.

She patted my head. "I admire your dreams," she said, "but you need to live in the real world and get rich."

"You just don't get it," I said.

My mom sighed. "Why can't you be more like your friend John. He is already operating his own souvenir shop at Scavenger Hunt stop no. 7. His mother told me he makes 25 emeralds per day."

"What is the use of money if you can't enjoy life?"

My mom shook her head. "Wait until your father gets home. He'll talk some sense into you."

My dad came home a few minutes later. He owned a store that sold maps of all the dead zombie locations.

And, as a direct descendant of the great zombie killer, my father wrote a biography of my great-great gramps that just about every tourist who came to our village purchased. The book was called: *Cornelius: Bane of Zombies*.

After my mom explained that I wanted to be a surfer, my dad sat down on the couch next to me and put his hand on my knee.

"Son, you can't make any emeralds surfing. Villagers need emeralds to survive," he said calmly.

I shook my head. "No, we need food and shelter to survive."

Cornelius

Bane of
Zombies

My dad smiled. "Well, how do you think you get that? You have to pay for it with emeralds."

"Do I?" I asked. "What about all these players who come to our world with nothing but their hard fists and a determined attitude? They seem to be able to survive without emeralds."

I don't think my dad saw that coming. It was a good point.

"Um, true, but they are not villagers. Villagers need emeralds. It is how it has always been."

"That is not a reason," I said. "What if I *could* get food and shelter *and* surf? Would that be okay?"

My dad sighed. He knew I would not give up.

"I'll tell you what, Jimmy. I will give you one month to prove to me that you can provide your own food and shelter while surfing. If you can do that, then maybe we can figure out a way for you to make some emeralds surfing too."

I smiled. I saw my mom frown. "Thanks, Dad!"

My dad patted my knee. "Now, go to bed and get some sleep. You have a lot of work to do in the next month."

Day 2 – Morning

I woke up today feeling happy. My dad was going to let me go surfing, for one month at least.

I put my hands behind my head and imagined all the awesome waves I would surf, all the places I would go, all the tubes I would get.

And, then, I had a horrible realization: *I didn't know how to surf!*

I sat up in a panic.

I had to get to the beach.

I had to get a surfboard.

I got out of bed and put on a pair of shorts. Then, I put my robe on over them.

I rushed into the kitchen and grabbed a loaf of bread.

"See you later, Mom," I shouted. "I'm going surfing."

I ran as fast as I could down to the ocean. As I ran, I tore chunks of bread from the loaf and gulped them down. Our village was only about a ten minute walk to the beach. I ran so fast that I made it there in three minutes.

I stood on the beach for a moment, taking in the beauty.

Today, I become a surfer, I thought.

I took off my robe and let it fall to the ground. The sun warmed my un-tanned villager skin. *Soon*, I thought, *I will look like a bronze statue like the surfers in the magazine.*

I stretched my arms and legs.

I was ready to go.

And, then, I realized: I didn't have a surfboard!

I sat down on the beach and started to cry. My dreams were destroyed. As far as I knew, no villager in the entire world even knew how to surf, much less build a surfboard. I couldn't even buy a surfboard with all the emeralds in the world because no one sold them.

I cried for about five minutes.

When I was done feeling sorry for myself, I thought, *WWSD?* (Which, if you don't know, means *What would Steve do?*)

Steve was the name of a very smart and resourceful player who had lived near our village last year. He helped keep zombies away, and we provided him with free food and other helpful items.

Me and the other village kids had watched him craft all sorts of things using only his crafting table and his imagination.

That's it! I will craft a surfboard!

From what I could tell by looking at the surf magazine, surfboards were basically like short planks. I guessed they must be made out of wood, though most of them seemed to be colored, so it was hard to tell exactly what they were made of.

I ran back to my house, and pulled my crafting table out from my closet. I went to the garage and found a block of big oak wood. I put it on the crafting table and, before you could say "Notch," I had a perfect plank.

A surfboard.

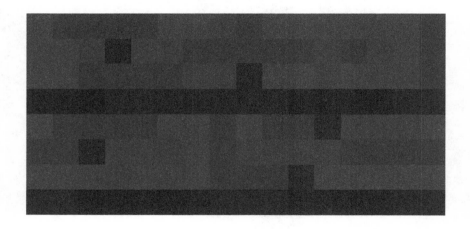

I took my sweet new board back to the beach.

I took off my robe and was getting ready to paddle out when I realized something else: *There weren't any waves!*

Day 2 – Afternoon

I've been sitting at the beach for hours, just staring at the flat, motionless water. My dream of becoming a surfer was dead.

How could I be a surfer if there weren't any waves to surf?

Suddenly, I heard some footsteps behind me. I turned around, fearing it was a creeper, but it was just a player.

"I don't have anything to trade, bro," I said. "Go away."

The player approached. He was a big, tall guy with blonde hair. "What are you doing down here?" he asked.

"I was going to surf," I said sadly.

The player smiled and looked excited. "Really? I didn't know there was surf in the oceans of the Overworld."

I laughed bitterly. "There isn't. I just realized it."

"Bummer," said the player. "I surf back in my world, and was hoping maybe surfing was a new thing here."

The player's words pulled me from my depression. "Wait. You surf?"

The player nodded. "Yeah, surfing is awesome."

I stood up and brushed the sand off my shorts. "Uh, could you teach me how to surf?"

"Well, I could, if there were some waves, but ...," he said, shrugging his shoulders.

"Yeah, well, there aren't," I spat, kicking the sand.

The player rubbed his chin in thought. Then, I could tell by his expression that he had an idea. "You know," he said, "I could teach you to SUP."

"SUP?"

"Stand Up Paddle," he explained. "It's kind of like surfing, but not really. You can do it without waves."

"Seriously?!?!??! That would be awesome!"

The player quickly crafted a plank, and then cut it into a smaller piece of wood. It was narrow at the top and wide at the bottom.

Then, he grabbed my surfboard and put it on the water.

"Okay, watch this."

I watched in awe as he stepped onto the surfboard with one foot. Then, just as he pushed off from the beach with the other foot, he put his paddle into the water and stroked.

With both feet on the surfboard, he deftly maneuvered it with the paddle. He went out into the ocean, and then paddled back to the shore.

He handed me the paddle. "You try," he said. "Just remember, getting the balance right is a bit tricky."

I was too excited to be careful. I put one foot on the board, pushed off with the other foot, and ... promptly fell into the water.

The player laughed as he helped me to my feet. "Keep trying. You'll get the hang of it soon."

"Okay," I said.

"Look, I need to take off and do some mining. I'll be back in a few days to check on your progress."

"Thanks," I said. "By the way, what is your name?"

"Laird. What's yours?"

"Jimmy. Jimmy Slade."

Day 3

I had worked on my SUP technique all day yesterday. By the end of the day, I had almost got the balance right, but it got dark and I had to come home before the zombies started roaming around.

Today, I woke up at first light and rushed down to the ocean with my board and paddle.

After a couple more hours of trying, I was able to balance and paddle wherever I wanted.

I paddled for hours. My arms ached with the effort.

But, it was so awesome.

Being in the ocean alone...

I could look down into the water and see squids swimming peacefully.

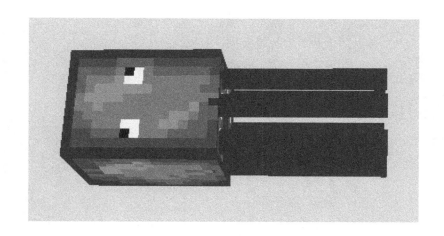

I could see schools of fish.

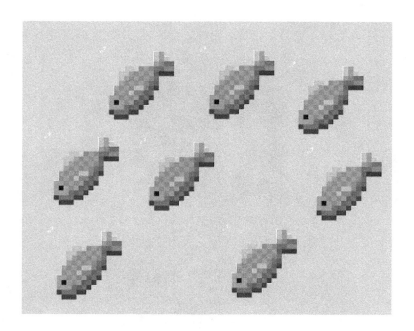

Now, if only I could find some waves....

Day 4 – Morning

The next morning, I ate breakfast and grabbed my surfboard and paddle, intending to go to the beach.

Just as I stepped outside my door, Biff stepped in front of me. "What's all that stuff?" he asked.

I don't like Biff very much. Heck, I didn't like him at all.

He is big and strong and mean. He is a bully.

His parents own the souvenir stand at the entrance to our village, so they make a lot of emeralds. The tourists buy maps and food from them on the way into the village and shirts, books (even my dad's book), plaques, posters and other knick-knacks on the way out.

I once heard my parents say Biff's parents are the richest people in the village.

Because his parents are rich, Biff thinks that he is entitled to tell all the other kids what to do. Unfortunately, he is also very strong, so if you don't do what he says, he punches you in the arm.

"This is my surfboard," I said, knowing that he was going to insult me no matter what I said, so I might as well tell the truth.

"Surfboard?" he said, raising the edge of his lip with a snarl. "Like cowabunga? gnarly dude? killer brah? That kind of surfboard?"

"I guess so."

"What a loser," he said, shoving me. "Don't you know there aren't any waves around here?"

"I can still SUP."

"SUP? 'Ssup with you, dork?"

I sighed. "It means Stand Up Paddle, not 'what's up'."

Biff laughed as he pulled the wooden paddle from my grip. "Let me guess. You stand on the surfboard and paddle around with this?"

"Yeah, it's fun," I said.

"Doesn't sound like surfing to me," said Biff. "Sounds more like canoeing without a boat."

I grabbed the paddle back. "Shut up. You just don't know how awesome it is. Besides, you are right. There aren't any waves here, so it's the best I can do."

I was so angry, I could feel tears coming to my eyes. Not because of what Biff said or did, but because I knew that I would never be able to be a real surfer without some waves.

Biff could tell I was getting really upset. I knew what he was thinking: Should I keep messing with him or should I find some other wimpy villager to pick on?

This was the make-or-break moment for Biff. If he miscalculated and sent me over the edge, I might freak out and do something he was not expecting. Bullies hate the unexpected; they like to control the situation. Biff decided to move on.

"Whatever," he said dismissively. "Enjoy splashing in the puddles, baby."

As I watched Biff lumber off to find another kid to torment, I realized I was starting to hyperventilate because I was so upset.

I needed to get to my happy place.

I needed to get to the beach.

Day 4 – Afternoon

I spent the rest of the morning paddling around on the ocean.

I paddled along the shoreline for a great distance, hoping to find some waves.

Nothing.

I don't understand.

The ocean in the world where the players came from had tons of waves. The pictures in my surf magazine proved it. Why aren't there waves in the oceans of my world?

I assumed there must be a scientific explanation for it. But, I have never been very good in science at school.

I remember this one time the science teacher at our school, Mrs. Drake, asked me to explain to the class what gravity was.

All I could say was: "It's the 'it' gravy. You know, fashionable. That's why they put 'it' inside the gravy."

I thought it was funny...

Mrs. Drake told me I needed to study more and that I could do it in the principal's office.

Since I needed a scientific explanation, I needed to talk to my friend, Emma. Emma was a whiz in science. She was always making all sorts of amazing things with redstone and levers and pistons and tracks.

One time, she built a small shack and put pressure plates inside so that every step you took made a different part of the interior glow. It was really cool. All the kids wanted to use it.

Biff told Emma she should charge an emerald to each kid to use it. I know I would have paid an emerald to use it. But, she refused to charge kids for something she built for fun.

Biff told her she was stupid. She told Biff he would have to pay five emeralds to use her glow house. He got all mad and left.

BEFORE　　　**AFTER**

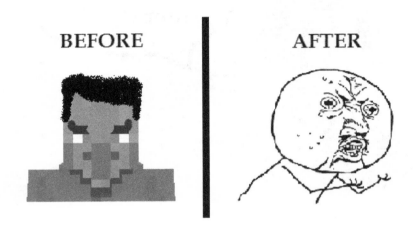

When I got to Emma's house, she was standing in her front yard staring at the trunk of a tree.

"Hey, Emma, what's up?" I said.

"Shhh," she said, putting a finger to her lips. "I am observing the bark."

O...kay.....

"Um, why do you need silence to look at bark?"

She sighed and turned away from the bark to look at me. "Silence helps me think."

"Oh, sorry," I said. "Maybe I can give you a new problem to think about?"

"Do you need the recipe for 'it' gravy?" she asked with a smile.

I laughed. "Do you have one?"

"If I did, I'd give it to my parents so they could sell gravy to tourists who visit their restaurant."

"Cool," I said. "Anyway, I have a problem, and I think science might have the answer."

Emma sat down on a stair leading up to the front door of her house. "What's the problem?"

I told her about my dream of surfing and the problem of no waves. I showed her a copy of my magazine with surfing pictures in it so she would understand what sorts of waves I was looking for.

Emma closed her eyes and leaned back, pondering for a few minutes. I was careful not to interrupt the silence of her thinking.

Finally, she opened her eyes and sat up slowly. "I think I might have an idea. I'll need to do some calculations.... It might take a few days.... Yeah, it might work."

I was SUPER-excited. "What? Tell me. What is the idea?"

Emma's eyes darted back and forth nervously and she rubbed her hands together. "Um, I ... well ... I don't think you'd understand. No offense."

I sighed. "That's okay. You are probably right. Unless it involves gravy, I'm sure it's over my head."

Emma smiled. "If my idea works, the waves are going to be over your head."

Day 5

I stopped by Emma's house first thing in the morning to check on her progress. She told me to get lost.

Mad scientist.

I went back home.

My mom asked me how the surfing was coming along.

I told her great. I'd be surfing and making emeralds in no time.

She patted my head like a dog.

I knew she didn't believe me.

The sad part is, I didn't believe me either. Unless Emma's idea worked, I'd never be a real surfer.

I decided not to go to the beach that day. Instead, I looked through my surfing magazine over and over, wishing I had waves.

"O great Notch," I said aloud. "Why did you not create waves when you created the world?"

"Because you are a lame dork," came the reply.

I sat up in my bed. Had I really just spoken with Notch?

But, I quickly realized I was wrong as I heard the laughter coming through my window.

I looked out the window and saw Biff walking away.

"You're mean," I yelled at him.

"At least I am not a surfer noob who will be a noob all his life because he will never learn to surf because there are no waves. Noob," said Biff with a big smile.

I didn't bother to reply. Unless Emma came up with a brilliant solution, Biff was right.

Day 6 – Morning

I stopped by Emma's house first thing in the morning to find out how she was doing.

Her mom told me that she was in her room working on a project and did not want to be disturbed for any reason.

I took that as a good sign. If she needed total isolation, she must be on to something.

I thanked her mom and went back to my house to grab my board and paddle. I thought I would SUP all day, and then check back with Emma in the evening.

After grabbing my board, paddle and some snacks, I walked down to the ocean. As I crested the final hill in the path, I saw something that made me furious.

Biff and some of his friends were in the water ... on SUPs!

I ran down to the edge of the ocean.

"What are you doing?!?" I shouted. "This is my beach."

Biff and his friends laughed.

"You don't own the ocean, Jimmy," said Biff. "We want to SUP too."

The ocean was my peaceful place and Biff and his posse were ruining it.

"Go somewhere else, then. This is my spot," I said.

They all laughed again. "No. We like this spot," said Biff.

I had never hated anyone more in my life than the way I hated Biff at that moment.

I thought about paddling out and pushing them all off their boards, but they would just wait for me on the shore and beat me up when I came in.

I sighed.

"Fine," I said. "But when I start surfing on real waves, you aren't invited."

"That'll be the day," said Biff.

I walked down the beach and around a hill. I wanted to find a spot where I could not see those idiots.

I realized that they were right about the ocean being open to everyone. But, I had basically invented a whole new way to enjoy the ocean, and they had stolen it for themselves.

I suppose I should be flattered they liked it, but it did not make me glad that I had to share the ocean with them.

I put my board in the water and then began to paddle. As I fell into a rhythm, I began to calm down.

The water beneath me was very clear. I could see the bottom, even though it was many blocks deep.

Did waves come from down there? Does our world lack some wave generating mineral that is present in the world where the players come from?

I hoped Emma could figure it out soon....

Day 6 – Evening

I paddled until I saw the sun setting. I stayed so late that I saw a zombie wandering toward my village just as I got to my house.

That is what I call cutting it close!

When I opened the door, my mom said, "Jimmy. Thank Notch. I was getting worried about you."

"Yeah, maybe I did stay out a bit late," I admitted. "Sorry, Mom."

She smiled. "It's okay. Get cleaned up and eat some dinner."

I went to the bathroom and washed my face.

I looked in the mirror. I was getting very tan from all the SUPing. It was nice to be outside all day long.

When I got back to the table, my parents were both sitting down. My mom had set out a dinner of steak, watermelon, bread and mushroom stew.

I was so hungry from all my exercising that I ate two steaks, one loaf of bread, three bowls of mushroom stew and an entire watermelon.

"Busy day?" asked my dad, noticing the unusually large amount of food I had consumed.

I shrugged. "Surfing is good exercise."

My mom snapped her figures. "That reminds me. Emma stopped by just before you got home. She said she had an idea about your surfing."

I stood up quickly. "Why didn't you tell me?"

"Slipped my mind."

"Arrgh," I said. "I'll see you later. I'm going to Emma's house."

"Take a torch and be careful of the hostile mobs," said my dad.

I grabbed a torch from the wall, ignited it, and rushed out the door.

***

I had to ditch one zombie and a skeleton on the way, but there was no real danger.

When I got to Emma's house, I banged on the door. Her father answered with an iron sword in his hand.

"Oh, hi, Jimmy," he said once he recognized me. "I thought maybe you were a zombie."

"Not yet, Mr. Watson," I said with a smile and a laugh.

Emma's father stepped aside and let me in. "Emma's in her room. She said to send you in if you came for a visit."

"Thanks," I said, quickly walking to her room.

I knocked on the door, and Emma said, "Come in."

I opened the door. Emma was sitting at her desk looking at a book.

"Jimmy!" she said as she jumped up from her desk and ran to hug me.

"Uh, hi," I said, pretending to hug her back. *Why do girls like to hug so much anyway?*

"I think I figured it out," she said with a smile as bright as the sun.

"Really? You mean, I can surf real waves?"

She nodded. "All we need are 40 wooden planks, six pistons, some redstone and one on-off lever."

My hopes were dashed.

"Is that all?" I asked sarcastically. "Where are we supposed to get all that stuff?"

"Seriously?" she asked, like I was stupid or something.

"Yeah, that stuff costs a lot."

Emma laughed. "We can harvest the wood in the forest, no problem. I actually have like 20 pistons and 30 redstone blocks in the storage shed in the back yard that are leftover from other experiments. And, I've got some levers in my room."

I was surprised. This girl really liked her science. "Wow. Awesome!"

"The hard part will be finding a place with the right bathymetry," she said.

"Uh, what?"

"*Bathymetry*. Just a fancy word for the bottom of the ocean," Emma explained. "We need to find a spot that goes from deep to shallow quickly and at a constant rate. That will make tubes."

I smiled, remembering what I had seen on my SUP earlier today. "I think I know the place. I'll show you tomorrow."

Day 7

The next morning, I met Emma at her house just as the sun was coming up. We wanted to get to the beach before Biff and his band of bullies showed up. We did not want them to see what we were doing.

We walked along the shore until we got to the location where I had SUPed yesterday.

I put my board in the water and told Emma to sit on it.

"Are you sure I won't fall in?" she asked.

"No, I am not sure, but I am getting pretty good at this. You should be alright."

Emma nodded and sat down on the SUP. I put my right foot on the board and then pushed off with my left. We drifted smoothly into the flat ocean.

I paddled Emma around for about 30 minutes so that she could observe the bottom of the ocean for herself. When she was satisfied by what she had seen, she said, "Let's get to the shore."

When we got to the shore, I asked Emma if she thought she could make some waves at this location.

"Totally. The hard part is going to be transporting the pistons to the other side of the water."

"Why are we going to do that?" I asked.

"Because we need the pistons over there to push the water over here."

"Why?"

Emma shook her head like I was the most dense block in the mine. "When you push a bunch of water at once, it ripples through the ocean. When it hits the shallow part, it will make a breaking wave."

"Really?"

She nodded. "Watch."

Emma picked up a small rock and tossed it into the water about 2 blocks from shore. I noticed as little ripples formed in the water.

"Wow, that's – "

"Shhh," she said. "Keep watching."

I watched as the ripples got closer to shore and then, just before they hit the edge of the water, they formed tiny breaking waves and slapped against the sand.

"Oh my Notch," I said. "Waves!"

"Imagine how big it will be with six pistons pushing 40 wooden planks through the water."

"You are awesome, Emma!"

She smiled. "Yeah, tell me something I don't know."

We talked about how to get all the pistons and planks down here without Biff or his friends seeing it. I did not want them to take over this part of the ocean before we built the wave machine.

We decided that tomorrow morning, Emma would borrow a horse cart from her mom and bring all six pistons to this area. We would dig a small cave and hide them inside. Then, each morning I could transport one or two pistons across the water.

Meanwhile, I would harvest trees for the wood needed to make the 40 planks. If anyone saw what I was doing, I would tell them I was going to make and sell SUPs. (Which actually is not a bad business idea....)

Once the pistons were in place and the planks attached, all we had to do was flip the activation lever, and the redstone would activate the pistons and start making waves.

We decided to put our plan into place tomorrow morning. I peeked around the hill and saw Biff and his pals in the water.

"Looks like we'll have to go the long way home," I said. "I don't want those guys coming over here and nosing around."

"That's okay," said Emma. "Maybe we can find some apples to pick on our way back to the village."

Day 8

Emma delivered the six pistons at first light and then took the horse cart home before anyone else got to the beach. I managed to transport two of them across the water on my SUP.

I spent the rest of the day on the other side of the ocean harvesting trees to turn into planks. I crafted just over twenty planks, which I piled behind some trees so no one could see them from the water.

Day 9

I transported two more pistons across the water without being seen. I made the rest of the planks.

I told Emma she should be ready to build her device tomorrow. She was happy. So was I.

Day 10 – Morning

I transported the final two pistons across the water. Emma went the long way around on her horse, Ada, arriving just as I was unloading the final piston.

"Well, it's all here," I said. "Now, you just have to build it."

"No problem," Emma said confidently, already beginning to move the parts into position.

"Need any help?"

She shook her head. "I prefer to do this sort of thing alone."

"Fine by me," I said as I leaned back against a tree trunk and fell asleep.

Day 10 – Afternoon

"Wake up, Jimmy. Wake up," said Emma as she kicked her foot softly against my ribs.

"I'm up."

"It's done," she said with a smile.

I sat up quickly. I looked out into the ocean and saw ... nothing.

"Where is it?"

"Underwater, of course."

I scratched my head. "So, how do we use it?"

Emma pointed. "See that locked chest?"

I nodded.

"We just open it and press the lever to activate the pistons."

"Did you try it yet?" I asked.

"No, I wanted you to have the honors." She handed me a key to the chest.

I walked over to the chest and unlocked it. Inside, I saw a small lever. The lever was connected to some redstone. I assumed the redstone led from the chest underground and then underwater to the pistons.

"How did you build all this so fast?" I asked.

Emma shrugged. "I've built lots of things. This was not very complicated actually."

"So, I just move the lever?"

"Yes, move it up and then return it to its original position."

"Here goes nothing," I said as I raised and then lowered the lever.

At first, nothing happened. I looked over at Emma. She did not seem worried.

Then, I heard a low groaning sound as the pistons came to life. It grew louder and louder, as if I had awakened some sort of beast from the depths of the sea.

And, I had.

I watched in awe as a huge bulge of water rose in the middle of the ocean and began moving toward the opposite shore. It … was … a … wave!

"You did it Emma," I shouted. "You did it!"

"Keep watching," she said, a huge grin spreading across her face.

I saw as the mountain of water got bigger and bigger and longer and longer. It was spreading out like a line in the water, just like the pictures I had seen in the surf magazine.

And then, suddenly, the center of the line creased and I saw a huge tower of white water erupt where the wave was crashing down into the ocean. I kept watching as the white water emerged in both directions of the wave.

What did they call this in the surf magazine…? An A-frame.

I could not believe it.

I grabbed my board and tossed it into the ocean, leaving my ridiculous paddle on the shore. I tossed the key to the chest to Emma.

"Let me get out there, and then you send another wave my way," I said, more excited than I had ever been in my entire life.

"You got it, Jimmy," said Emma.

I paddled as fast as I could into the middle of the water. I looked back at Emma and waved. I saw her move the lever up and down.

Then, I watched as a gigantic lump of water made its way toward me. I turned around and paddled as fast as I could, trying to get into position to catch the wave.

Since I had never caught a wave before, I really had no idea what to do.

I turned around and saw the wall of water closing in on me. I paddled faster and faster and …. Suddenly, I was moving without paddling. I had caught the wave!

I scrambled to my feet and was cutting along the face of the wave. I could feel the wind in my hair.

I was surfing!

The images from the magazine flooded into my mind.

What should I do?

Should I turn?

Should I try to get in the tube?

The wave decided for me as it suddenly pitched over me and I found myself inside the wave, completely pitted, piped and barreled. I was in the tube.

I gave a shout of joy.

This was amazing. Indescribable. How was I even doing this on my first wave?

Then, I felt air sucking into the barrel.

What?

And, then, I heard a roaring sound behind me and a huge bang like a cannon roared past me. It lifted me off my board and shot me out of the barrel.

I'm a bird!

And then I landed with a *SPLAT* in the water. It kind of hurt.

I found my board floating nearby and climbed on top of it. I sat on my board, watching the final section of the wave break just in front of the shore.

It was then that I noticed Biff and his buddies standing on the shore, staring at me in silent disbelief.

Oh, great, I thought.

Then, I noticed Laird was standing there too. He was making a strange hooting noise, like he had completely lost his mind.

Laird grabbed the board from Biff and paddled out to me.

"Dude, that was so awesome!" he said. "What a sick pit!"

"I didn't make it out though," I said. "Not on my board anyway."

"So what?" he said. "Can I ride one?"

"Yeah," I said. "Let's paddle back to the take off spot."

We got back and waved at Emma who cranked the lever up and down.

"You go left," said Laird, "and I'll go right."

Day 11

The next morning, Emma and I went back to the beach. There were already 50 villagers waiting for us, most of them kids.

Insta-crowd.

I took Emma across the water on my SUP so that she could operate the wave machine.

Then, I paddled toward the take off spot. I saw Laird paddling out from shore.

The kids on the shore waved at me and Laird as we paddled to the take off spot. They watched in awe as we rode some waves.

After a few waves, I paddled to shore and was surrounded by kids.

"Can I ride one?"

"Will you make me a board?"

"How much for a surf lesson?"

And, suddenly, I realized how I could surf and make money.

My parents would be proud of me for earning emeralds and I could do something I loved every day for the rest of my life.

At least, I hope that is how it works out....

END of Book 1

DIARY OF A SURFER VILLAGER

Book 2

(an unofficial Minecraft book)

Day 12 – Morning

I woke up today with the biggest smile EVER on my face because yesterday was so awesome!

Everyone thought the wave that Emma and I had created – well, Emma really had done all the creating, but I put her up to it – was cool. They all wanted to learn how to surf.

I was making plans already on how to make money from the wave and to still be able to surf it every day. My dream of making a living from surfing was becoming real!!!

I got dressed and went downstairs to eat breakfast. Mom had cooked some pork chops and apple pie. Apple pie is my favorite breakfast, but I was so excited and distracted that I could barely eat. My parents noticed.

"So, I heard the wave machine was a big success," said my dad.

I nodded as rapidly as an enthusiastic puppy. "Totally. Everyone wants to ride it. I'm going to set up a surf shop and surf school and earn tons of emeralds. I told you I could make a living surfing!"

My dad smiled. "You did. I have to admit that I did not believe you, but I am proud of you for realizing your dream."

"Don't forget to share half of your money with Emma," added my mom. "Without her, none of this would be happening."

I hadn't really thought about sharing my emeralds, but I didn't mind. My mom was right. Emma was the brains behind this operation.

"I guess sometimes selfish dreams can only be realized through teamwork with others," I said with a trance-like voice in a sudden moment of Zen-like clarity.

My parents looked at me curiously. I don't think they had expected this answer. Maybe a "sure" or "no way," but not a deep thought like this. (At least, I thought it was a deep thought that I had thought, was it not?)

"True," said my dad. "We will have a difficult time running our souvenir shop without you, but I am sure we can hire another one of the villager kids to help with the summer tourist rush."

I had not thought about how my dreams would impact my parents. They gave me food and a home for twelve years of my life, and now I was going out on my own ... business-wise anyhow.

"Gee, dad, I'm sorry. I could still help out in the evenings, when it is too dark to surf."

My dad shook his head. "No. Building a business is hard work. You will be tired at the end of the day."

"Besides," added my mom, "there is only one more month of summer vacation. After that everyone will have to go back to school, so your dad and I can manage the store during the slower months of the year."

Oh my Notch! I hadn't thought of that. Once the summer season was over, the tourist stream would dry up and it would just be the local village kids. I couldn't make a living just from them! Could I?

"Only one more month of summer? Oh, no. That won't give me much time to earn mass stacks of emeralds," I said in a whiney voice.

"Hmmm," said my dad, rubbing his chin in thought. "Sounds like you've built yourself a seasonal business there, Jimmy my boy."

"Is that bad?"

"Not necessarily, but you will need to make most of your money during a small window of time."

I sighed. Total bummer.

"Unless, of course, you can think of a way to keep selling things to people during the off season," suggested my mom.

I snapped my head and looked at my mom with wide eyes. "What do you mean?"

She shrugged. "Figure out something surfers will buy all year round, even when there is no surf or they can't travel to your wave."

"Like what?" I asked, desperate for knowledge and ideas.

"I have no idea," she said. "It's your business."

I sighed again as I stood up from the table. "Well, guess I better go start earning."

My mom nodded. "Jimmy, you also might want to think about how you will run your business when you go back to school in one month. The tourists will be gone, but the local kids will still want to surf."

I sighed yet again. "I'm not sure I can go to school *and* run a business."

"I'm not sure you can either," said my mom, "but, if it matters enough to you, you will try."

I smiled, buoyed by my mom's attempt to make me feel better. *Maybe I could do it?* And, if I couldn't, at least I could still make money during the summer.

"Thanks, mom. I need to get going. Customers are waiting."

"That's my boy," said my dad, slapping me on the back as I walked away from the table.

As I walked out the door, I sang softly to myself, "Every day, I be hustlin', hustlin', hustlin'."

Day 12 – Afternoon

"Okay, everyone. We are going to shut the wave machine down for about thirty minutes for a maintenance check!" I announced to the crowd of about one hundred young villagers in or near the water.

"Ah, man!"

"Lame."

"Weak."

I laughed at how entitled these kids felt after just one day of having access to the first surfable wave in the Overworld.

I grabbed my SUP, put a chest of food on it, and paddled to the other side of the ocean where Emma was stuck operating the wave machine.

When I arrived, Emma smiled at me. "It gets kind of lonely over here. I think I need to craft a controller on the other side of the ocean."

I handed Emma the basket of food I had brought.
"Can you do that?"

Emma took the basket and looked inside. "Yum.
Roasted chicken and carrots. Thanks."

I nodded. "Well, can you do it?"

Emma chomped on a roasted chicken leg. "No
problem," she said with her mouth full. "I just need a

couple hours. If you can shut the wave down early today, I can build it in the evening."

I pointed across the ocean at the mass of villagers waiting for the waves to turn back on. "They aren't going to like it."

Emma shrugged. "They'll get over it. It's not like they can go surf somewhere else."

"I suppose," I said. "By the way, my parents mentioned something to me today about school starting in one month. I guess that means we'll have to shut the place down."

"Maybe, but we could still run it on the weekends. Maybe even after school a few days a week," suggested Emma.

I beamed at her. "You are brilliant."

Emma raised an eyebrow. "Nothing brilliant about it. Kinda obvious, really."

"We're business partners, right?" I asked.

"Sure," said Emma, crunching a carrot.

"Good, because I might know about surfing, but I don't know anything about making money."

Emma laughed. "Seems pretty easy so far. Anyway, after tonight, I'll be on the other side of the ocean with you in case you need any help."

I stood up and smiled. "I'm sure I will." I walked over to my SUP and picked up my paddle. "When I get to the middle of the ocean, turn on the machine. I want to get one barrel before the crowd paddles out."

"Sure thing, partner," said Emma, smiling.

Day 12 – Late Afternoon

I stood behind the counter where I collected emeralds from villagers wanting surf lessons or wanting to ride the wave. I counted two hundred emeralds already. Amazing!

But, I had to shut the wave down now. Emma needed daylight to build the redstone connector so we could operate the wave from this side of the ocean. I really didn't want to stop collecting emeralds. I bet I could have made another fifty before the sun set.

Sigh.

"Everyone! We have to shut the wave down for the day. Please paddle in and return your rented boards. Thank you for your, cooperation."

"Lame."

"Seriously, man?"

"Bogus."

I shook my head. How rude were these kids? At first, I thought it was just the tourists, but I saw some of the kids I went to school with making rude comments, too. I won't name names, since they might read this diary, but let's just say they were some of the more popular kids.

Emma heard the announcement and shut down the wave. The kids paddled in and returned their boards, giving me evil looks as they did.

"We open again tomorrow at 9:00 a.m," I said.

"Whatever."

"So what?"

Hooray for you."

"And, the first thirty people in line get in for free," I said.

"Epic!"

"Sweet!"

"Notch-tastic!"

Maybe I could be a businessman after all?

I watched as the kids walked back to town. They were all sunburnt and tired. I bet they slept well tonight.

I looked across the ocean and saw Emma already diving into the water to build the redstone connector. When she surfaced, I yelled, "Do you need any help?"

"No," she yelled back.

"Okay," I shouted. "I'll hang out until you are done."

Emma waved and dove back into the water. Emma sure was awesome. None of this would exist without her. *Maybe I should give her more than half of the emeralds we earn?*

I checked to make sure that I had gathered all of the emeralds and then put them into a locked chest that was inside a larger locked chest inside a still larger locked chest.

"The best in villager security," I said proudly looking at the chest.

Emma worked quickly, completing the redstone connector well before the sun set. She emerged from the ocean soaking wet. I brought her a beach towel.

"Thanks," she said as she dried off.

"All done?"

She shook her head like a wet dog. The spray from her hair soaked my robe. "Knock it off," I whined.

Emma laughed. "I just need to make the final connection, and we can test it."

Emma crafted a lever and placed it behind the counter. Then, she placed some redstone and connected it to the redstone in the ocean. She slapped her hands together. "Done."

"Cool."

"Want to do the honors, Jimmy?"

I nodded and reached over and flipped the lever. The ocean roared to life and the waves rolled toward shore. It still took my breath away. A perfect A-frame wave with tubes in both directions.

"Awesome," I said.

"Do you mind if I paddle out and try to catch a few?" asked Emma. "I haven't had a chance yet."

Wow, what a selfish jerk I had been!

"Sure. Do you need a lesson?"

Emma shook her head. "It seems pretty simple, at least in concept."

I flipped the lever to turn off the waves. Emma paddled out and stopped at the takeoff spot. She waved her arm, indicating she was ready. I turned on the machine.

She tried to catch the first wave, but it passed under her.

"Paddle harder!" I yelled.

Emma did, and she caught the second wave. She got to her feet, wobbled for a precarious moment, and then shifted her weight and trimmed along the face of the wave. She had an expression of pure joy and stoke.

"Yeah!" I yelled.

"Who-hoo," screamed Emma as she rode the wave all the way to shore.

She ran onto the beach and right up to me and hugged me tight.

I still don't understand what it is with girls and hugging.

"That was so much fun!" she said.

"You are preaching to the choir, buddy."

Emma looked back at the ocean as the waves rolled in. "It is going to be hard to stand behind the counter and watch everyone else having fun tomorrow."

I nodded. "Maybe we can take turns going out there?"

"That would be cool," said Emma.

"Ahh, how cute," said a mean voice, dripping with sarcasm. It could have been only one person. Emma and I turned around and confirmed its source: Biff.

"What do you want, Biff?" I asked, spitting the words from my mouth.

"Just wanted to let you know that I've opened a SUP school around the corner," he said with a grin.

I laughed. "So what? SUPing is lame compared to surfing."

Biff smiled. "Maybe. And maybe that is why I only charge one emerald for all-day SUP rental, lesson, lunch, and babysitting."

"And, why are you telling us that?" asked Emma.

"Just wanted to let you know why you won't have any customers tomorrow," he said with an evil grin spreading across his face. "Ta-ta."

I stared at Biff's back thinking of all the violent things I could do to him, but which would ultimately fail because he would beat me up. I shook my fist at him, but said nothing.

"Come on," said Emma. "Forget about him. Besides, we need to get home. The sun is starting to set."

I looked at the sky. Emma was right. We needed to get home to avoid the zombies. I'd figure out what to do about Biff later.

Day 13 – Morning

I woke up today with the biggest frown EVER.

Stupid, Biff.

He was trying to steal my customers. He was just jealous of the mad wealth I was going to make. He couldn't let me just have my fun. A true bully in all aspects of his pathetic life.

I brushed my teeth and then pulled on my surfing shorts and then put my robe on. I stumbled down the stairs to the kitchen to eat breakfast. My parents were already there.

"How's business?" asked my dad.

"It was great yesterday, but now stupid Biff is opening a SUP school around the corner from my surfing beach. He'll probably steal all my customers."

"Didn't you mention the other day that surfing and SUPing were totally different?" asked my mom.

"I did, but that isn't entirely true. You get to be in the ocean on a board. You can even ride a wave with a SUP."

"Hmmm. Maybe he will grab a few customers at that," said my dad unhelpfully.

"What should I do?" I asked desperately.

My parents both shrugged and said at the same time, "It's your business. You figure it out."

"Seriously? No help at all?!?"

"Look, Jimmy, I don't know the first thing about surfing or surf culture. All I know is that if you offer people an experience they want, then they will pay for it. As long as people want to learn how to surf, you will have customers," said my dad.

"As long as Biff doesn't steal them all," I said in a sad, whiny voice.

My mom patted me on the head like a pet dog. "Jimmy. A little competition is necessary for the market to function. Look at how many restaurants and souvenir shops there are in our delightful village of Zombie Bane, and we all manage to make a living."

She had a point. There were so many tourists who came to our village, especially in the summer, that we were flush with emeralds.

"And," she added, "you have the only surfable wave in the entire Overworld. I think you'll be alright even if twenty SUP schools opened in town."

My mom was right. I needed to stop being such a wimpy villager and start seeing the positive side of things. If nothing else, I would probably make enough emeralds this summer to pay for a house when I was old enough to move out. I – and when I say "I," I mean Emma and I – had created a unique business. I would be okay.

But, look at my thought process. Emeralds, emeralds, emeralds! My villager genetics were showing their true colors. I was more worried about going out of business than about surfing. How had this happened in less than two weeks? Did wealth corrupt the mind? Was money the end of freedom?

I shook my head to clear it of these deep, intense, profound questions. I had no time to solve them. I needed to catch a few waves and then open the ocean for business.

I demolished a plate of scrambled eggs, devoured a cold pork chop, gobbled a slice of apple pie, and guzzled two glasses of milk.

"Got to go," I said as I stood up from the table and ran out the door as my parents smiled and waved.

As I ran along the path to the beach, I approached Biff's SUP school. Biff was already there with a couple of his brutish friends and a girl I did not recognize. She was tall, like Biff, and looked about the same age. She wore a strange, multicolored robe.

I put my hands in my robe pockets as I passed. I did not want to talk to anyone, though I was curious about the strange girl. But, of course, Biff would not let me pass in peace.

"Hey, dork, ready to go broke?" Biff taunted.

"No way that is going to happen. I made over two hundred emeralds yesterday. How many did you make?" I taunted right back.

Biff turned red. He hadn't made any emeralds, I am sure. But, I was equally sure he *would* make some emeralds today. The question was how many would he make and how many of those were emeralds I should have been making.

"Whatever, dude. We'll see who is ruling the roost at the end of the summer," said Biff.

Ruling the roost? Who uses farming idioms these days?

The girl turned to Biff and said, "Aren't you going to introduce us?"

I looked more closely at the girl's multicolored robe. I had never seen any of the girls wearing robes like that in our village. They just wore the standard, single-colored robes. In fact, now that I thought about it, I had never seen any villager of any age wearing a multi-colored robe.

Biff sighed. "Jimmy, this is my cousin, Claire Dretsky. Claire, this is a dork who lives in this village named Jimmy Slade."

Claire laughed and reached out her right hand. "Nice to meet you, Jimmy."

I took her hand and shook it. "Nice to meet you, too, Claire. Uh, by the way, where did you get that crazy robe?"

Claire let go of my hand and took a step back. She looked down at her robe and then back at me. She struck a pose with her hands on her hips like some sort of fashion model. "Oh, this little thing? I got it at a shop back in the City."

"The City?" I asked.

"Capitol City, duh," said Biff. "Claire lives there. She's just visiting for the summer."

Capitol City. Whoa!

Capitol City was the center of all culture and wealth in the Overworld. I had never been, but heard that it housed the pinnacle of villager power in the Overworld. It was where the government of the Overworld was centered. Sure, each village had its own mayor, but the different regions and biomes sent delegates to Capitol City to create laws and ensure order throughout Minecraft.

It was said that Notch himself designed the layout of the City and even built the building which housed the villager government.

It was also said that people who lived in Capitol City were the leaders of fashion and thought. Claire's multi-colored robe seemed to provide evidence that this was, in fact, true, at least as to the fashion part of that saying.

"So, are your parents in the government?" I asked, unable to disguise a slight tone of awe in my voice.

Claire shook her head. "No, they are merchants who import raw materials from the Nether. Very dangerous and very lucrative."

"Cool," I said. "I'd like to see the Nether someday."

Claire laughed. "I wouldn't. It sounds gross, hot and stinky."

I laughed too. I liked Claire. She was stylish and mysterious.

Just then, Emma walked up. "What's so funny?"

I shrugged and pointed at Claire, "Claire is."

"Claire?" said Emma, raising an eyebrow.

Claire reached out her hand. "Claire Dretsky. I'm Biff's cousin. And you are...?"

"Emma. Emma Watson. I live in town. I run the surf school with Jimmy."

"Good for you," said Claire. I thought I detected a hint of sarcasm in her voice, but I could not be sure.

Emma tapped her chin with one of her fingers and looked into the distance for a moment. "Dretsky. Dretsky." Emma snapped her fingers. "Are you related to the famous Dretsky family that developed the Nether portal technology a few hundred years ago?"

Claire smiled. "The very same, though I don't know anything about science. I prefer fashion."

Emma sighed. "That's too bad, I was hoping to pick your brain about a few concepts I've been working on."

"Talk to my brother, Clayton. He'll be here tomorrow. He's the nerd in the family."

"Great!" said Emma. Claire rolled her eyes.

"Come on, Emma. Let's get the beach ready for the flood of customers," I said, raising my voice toward the end of my sentence so that Biff was sure to hear how confident I was.

Biff laughed and shook his head, but did not say anything. I'm not sure why. Maybe he didn't want to look like a total bully in front of his cousin. Maybe he was setting us up for something. Or, maybe he just couldn't think of anything to say.

"Bye. Nice to meet you, Claire," I said.

"Likewise," said Claire.

Emma waved and we continued to the beach.

When we arrived, Emma and I each took off our robes. "Being able to work in a bathing suit is pretty awesome, huh?" said Emma.

"Totally," I said. "Let's paddle out and catch a few before the crowd gets here."

We each grabbed a surfboard and Emma flipped the lever to turn on the wave machine. It took a little longer to paddle out since we had to go under the white water from several waves.

We surfed for about thirty minutes and then rode one last wave to the shore.

When we walked up the beach, there were already fifty people in line.

Day 14 – Midday

Today was another great day. Lots of customers at the surf school. We made 150 emeralds before lunch time.

And then, we made even more money *during* lunch time because we had constructed a small snack shack Emma and I had planned. We sold apples, pork chops, cookies, and cakes to eat. We sold milk, water and apple juice to drink.

While Emma ran the snack shop, I stood at the entry gate to the surfing area. I saw a boy, maybe a couple years older than me, walking towards the entrance. He was wearing a strange, multicolored robe.

This must be Claire's brother, Clayton, I thought.

The boy strode confidently toward me and then stopped. "You Jimmy?"

I nodded. "You must be Clayton."

"Yep," he said, passing his eyes over the few structures we had built. Then, he noticed a wave pop up in the ocean and break. A look of amazement crossed his face as he watched a couple of villagers surfing on the wave. I could tell he was impressed.

"What do you think?" I asked.

He shrugged, trying to pretend he wasn't impressed by a rustic country villager like me. "Pretty cool, I guess. How does it work?"

"If I told you, I'd have to kill you," I said in a flat, serious voice.

Clayton looked at me in shock.

I laughed. "Just kidding. I have no idea. Emma," I said, pointing to where she was selling a cookie five-year-old with a salt water booger hanging out of his nose, "is the brains behind the operation. You should talk to her."

A strange, sly smile crossed Clayton's face. "I will do just that. Thanks, kid," he said as he walked off.

Kid?

I shrugged as I watched Clayton walk over to the snack shack where he leaned casually against it and struck up a conversation with Emma.

Emma smiled and giggled as she moved her hands in various ways, obviously explaining how the wave machine worked. When she had finished, Clayton bought two cookies and handed one to Emma.

Did she just blush?

Clayton left the snack shack and walked back to me as he chomped his cookie.

"Say, Jimmy?" he said.

"What?" I asked curtly. For some reason, I did not like Clayton very much. Was it his attitude of Capitol City superiority, the way he ate his cookie, or the way he spoke with Emma?

"How much for a surf lesson?"

"One emerald for thirty minutes. Or, you can pay two emeralds for a thirty minute lesson and then have access to the wave for the rest of the day."

Clayton dug into one of the pockets of his multi-colored robe and pulled out seven emeralds. He tossed two at me. "It looks like fun. I think I'll be here for a while."

I put the emeralds into the storage chest. "You can change into a bathing suit over there," I said, pointing to a dressing room. "I'll pick out a surfboard while you do that. Meet me at the edge of the water."

Clayton smiled smugly as he stuffed the five emeralds back into his robe. "Okay. See you in a minute."

As I watched Clayton walk away, I suddenly became angry. I knew his family was rich. I knew he thought he was better than me. Better than anyone in this village, probably.

It seemed weird that Claire could be so nice and Clayton so arrogant. But, maybe Claire was like that too, only she hid it better? After all, they were related to Biff, and I already knew what a jerk he was.

I really did not want to give Clayton a surf lesson, but I was running a business and he had paid so there was nothing I could do.

At that moment, Clayton emerged from the dressing room in a multi-colored pair of swimming trunks. He flexed his well developed muscles, pausing just long enough for all the girls on the beach to spot him and giggle. Then, he slowly walked over to where I was waiting for him by the edge of the water.

Are you kidding me with this guy?

When Clayton was standing right next to me, he said, "Let us begin."

As much as I thought Clayton was a tool, I had to admit he was extremely athletic. It only took a few minutes before he was standing up on the surfboard. By the end of the lesson, he could trim along the face of the wave.

And, by the end of the day, he was unleashing vicious turns, carves, and slashes. And, I even saw him get barreled a couple of times.

In short, he ripped. He was almost as good as I was. If he came back tomorrow, he would probably be better.

I hated him even more now.

Day 15 – Morning

I felt very *blah* when I woke up this morning, like I hadn't gotten enough sleep. My eyes were dry, like someone had dumped skeleton bone meal into them while I was asleep. I wanted to stay in bed all day.

I was just drifting back to sleep when I heard a loud banging. I sat up and tried to rub the sleep from my eyes.

"What is it?" I spat.

"Emma's here," said my mom, standing in the doorway and resting her hand on my bedroom door where she had been knocking. "She wanted to walk with you to the surfing park thingy ... or whatever it is you are calling your business."

It was then that I realized two things: (1) running a business can take over your life to the point where it runs you and (2) Emma and I needed to think of a cool name for the surfing park thingy.

"Okay," I muttered as I got out of bed.

My mom smiled. "Good. Now, get dressed. I'll pack you some breakfast to go."

"Thanks, mom," I said as she closed the door.

I changed into some board shorts and put on my robe. My plain, boring, brown robe. I wanted a cool multi-colored one like Claire and Clayton had. *Maybe, with all the emeralds I was making, I will buy one*, I thought.

"Superstar," I whispered aloud as I imagined parading through the village wearing my flashy new robe as everyone gawked at me. I smiled.

I left my room and walked into the living room. Emma was sitting on the couch reading a book.

"Hey," I said.

"Hey," said Emma, smiling.

"What are you reading?"

She laughed. "*Cornelius: Bane of Zombies*. It is actually pretty good. Your dad is not a bad writer."

I smirked. "Haven't you heard the story enough times in history class?"

Emma stood up and shrugged. "Yeah, but not in as much detail. Did you know that Cornelius killed one of the ten zombies with a fork?!?"

"I know every last detail in that book," I said with a sigh. And it was true. My dad read drafts of that book aloud to us over and over while he was writing it. The contents of the book were etched ... no ... they were *seared* into my brain.

"A fork," repeated Emma, shaking her head with amazement. "I guess our ancestors were made of much heartier stuff than we."

"Whatever," I said.

"Don't belittle your ancestors, Jimmy," chided my mom as she handed me a small chest. "I've packed a pork chop and apple pie for breakfast along with some milk that I put in an old potion bottle."

"Thanks, mom," I said as I opened the chest and grabbed the apple pie. I shoved the pie in Emma's direction. "Want some?"

Emma shook her head. "I already ate."

"Good," I said as I bit into the pie. "I'm starving."

"Good-bye, Mrs. Slade," said Emma as we walked out the door.

"Bye, mom," I said with my mouth full.

It was a beautiful day outside. The sun was shining. No clouds in the sky. A slight breeze to keep things from getting stagnant and humid.

I finished eating my apple pie and washed it down with a gulp of milk. As I licked the residue of apple pie filling from my fingers, I said, "Emma, we need to come up with a name for our surfing park thingy. Something rad and catchy."

"Good idea. What about … um … Surfing Safari?"

I shook my head. "Too exotic."

"Surf Retreat?"

"Too boring."

"iSurf?"

"Too copycat-ish."

"Super Epic Rad Barrel-Making Surf Machine Park?"

"Too stupid."

"Well, do you have any ideas?" asked Emma.

I shook my head. "Not really. Let me kick it around for a bit. I'll come up with something."

"Okay."

We were about halfway to the surf park thingy and I had just started eating my delicious pork chop when we ran into Biff and Claire.

"Hey, dorks," he said, offering his standard greeting.

"What?" I said. The pork chop suddenly tasted less delicious.

"Nothing. Just heading to Biff's SUP School and Pool to make some money," responded Biff.

I smiled at Claire briefly, but then returned the scowl to my face. I couldn't believe Biff had already thought of such a cool name for his SUP park thingy.

While I was lost in thought, Biff reached over and grabbed my pork chop. "This looks good."

I grabbed at the pork chop, but it was out of reach. "Give it back, you jerk!"

"But, I'm hungry," he said, taunting me with the pork chop just out of reach. "My mommy didn't pack me a lunch."

I could see Claire smiling, but at least she didn't laugh.

In the past, I would have kept jumping for the pork chop until Biff decided to eat it or toss it on the ground. But, this time, I realized that I had twenty emeralds in my robe pocket that I had forgotten about.

"Whatever, Biff. Go ahead and eat it. If your family can't afford to feed you breakfast, I feel sorry for you."

The look on Biff's face was priceless.

I turned my back and said, "Come on, Emma. Let's stop at the Potato Shack and get a hot breakfast. I'm buying."

Day 15 – Afternoon

It was another financially successful day at the surf park thingy. Ugh! I needed to come up with a good name, and fast.

Clayton showed up shortly after lunch, rented a surfboard, paddled out, and proceeded to rip the wave to shreds. I couldn't believe how good this guy was.

Everyone was watching him. The speed of his turns, the spray from his cutbacks, the ferocity of his bottom turns, and the insane deepness of his tube-riding.

I hated to admit it, but he was amazing. Well, as a surfer anyway. As a person, he left a lot to be desired. I'll give you an example.

After surfing for a couple hours, Clayton paddled in and sat on the beach. After he relaxed for a few minutes, he clapped his hands and yelled, "Jimmy! Jimmy!"

Was he yelling at me?

I walked slowly over to Clayton and asked, "What's up?"

"Bring me a carrot and apple smoothie."

"I'm not a waiter. You can go wait in line at the snack shack with everyone else."

"Get me the smoothie," he said with an insistent voice. "Here." He tossed three emeralds at me.

I tossed the emeralds back. I spoke through gritted teeth, "I'm not a waiter. Besides, smoothies only cost one emerald at the snack shack."

Clayton laughed and stood up, brushing the sand from his surf trunks. "If you aren't a waiter, you should hire one. No one wants to have to walk all the way to the snack shack for a post-surf drink. You'll never make it as a businessman, Jimmy-boy." Clayton turned and walked to the snack shack to buy his smoothie from Emma.

What a jerk! I thought as I kicked the sand. Still, he had a point about hiring a waiter. It might actually increase sales. But, I couldn't let him know he was right. I'd wait until he went back to Capitol City, then I would see about hiring a waiter.

I looked back at the ocean, seeking some peace of mind. The motion of the waves and the smell of the salt spray had an almost instantaneous calming effect on me.

Except for right now because I saw Biff and Claire riding their SUPs in my surf park thingy area.

I ran up the shore to where I kept my own SUP. I grabbed it and a paddle and rushed to the water. I jumped on top of my SUP and stroked furiously toward Biff and his cousin.

"Hey! Hey! What are you doing out here?" I yelled.

Biff just laughed. Claire looked confused.

"Biff said it was okay," she said apologetically. "We just paddled around the point from Biff's SUP School and Pool."

My face turned red with anger. "Biff, you know you can't use this wave without paying for it. Now, give me two emeralds or get lost."

Biff continued to laugh. "Listen to you. Your greedy villager soul rises to the top. Anger strips away the pretense of being a cool surfer bro, doesn't it?"

Was he right? Were emeralds the only thing I cared about?

"That's not true, Biff. I just don't like inconsiderate buffoons that have nothing better to do than to use things that don't belong to them."

Biff's laughter continued unabated. "Whatever, bro. Here," he said, pulling two emeralds from his bathing suit and tossing them at me.

I was so surprised that I didn't react in time, and the emeralds splashed into the water and sunk to the bottom of the ocean.

"Aren't you going in after them?" asked Biff. "They sure seemed important a second ago."

"Shut up and leave," I said angrily.

"No. I paid you."

"No, you didn't."

Biff paddled closer to me. Claire looked back and forth at us, wondering how this was going to be resolved.

Biff looked at me with a fierce gaze. The kind of look he got right before he pummeled a smaller kid. I'd seen it up close many times before. But, this time, I wasn't going to back down.

"You wanted two emeralds. I gave you two emeralds. It is not my fault you never learned how to catch, you little baby. Now, go away and let me and my cousin have some fun." Biff punctuated this request by prodding me in the chest with his SUP paddle.

Inside my brain, I was seeing red. Just red. Like my brain had become a sack filled with blood and hate. I knew that I was going to fight Biff. I knew that it was going to be rough. I knew that I was likely to lose, but I no longer had any choice in the matter. My scarlet brain had already decided for me. There was no logic to my thoughts, no planning. Just rage.

I felt my legs crouching slightly to prepare for the leap from my SUP to Biff's. And, just before I was going to launch myself at Biff, fate ... or maybe Notch ... intervened.

A school of about a dozen fish suddenly leapt from the water and slammed into Biff's chest. The force of the fish knocked him off his feet, and he fell into the water.

Biff came up from the water sputtering and spitting water. He held on to his SUP and panted for air.

I laughed hysterically at him, as my brain turned from angry red to a mirthful yellow. Claire laughed so hard, she fell off her SUP also.

As I stood there, standing on my SUP, looming down at Biff. My brain changed from a mirthful yellow to a calmed blue.

What was the point of fighting Biff? And, why had I been so angry in the first place?

"You know what, Biff? I'll let you and Claire use my wave today, free of charge. Here's your refund," I said, reaching into my surf trunks, grabbing two emeralds, and tossing them to Biff. Biff reached for them, but couldn't quite catch them. They sunk to the bottom of the ocean, joining the other two emeralds in the briny deep.

Day 16

Today was uneventful. The crowds kept coming, and Emma and I kept making tons of emeralds. I think we made more in a week than some adult villagers made in a year. No lie.

In fact, when I was walking to the surf park thingy – still haven't thought of a name – a few of the adult villagers were scowling at me. It wasn't fair to be jealous of a twelve-year-old, was it? And, what was the point of their jealousy? They had nothing to be jealous of. I mean, seriously, *they* didn't have to go to back to school in a few weeks like me, so what was there to be jealous about?

The only strange thing that happened today was when I saw Clayton on the opposite side of the ocean. He was walking along the shore, near where Emma's wave machine was.

Emma was standing next to me when I noticed Clayton. I tapped her shoulder and pointed. "What do you think he's up to?"

Emma shrugged. "When I explained to him the other day how the machine worked, he asked where it was. Maybe he just wants to see it in action? He is super interested in science."

"Maybe," I said, unconvinced. There was something about Clayton that just wasn't right. His sister Claire was a bit arrogant from living in the City, but otherwise okay. Clayton had something else going on, something darker. There was a sense of entitlement when he tried to order that smoothie from me, like his superiority was the obvious order of things.

Who knows, maybe there are lots of servants in the City and he is just used to it. After all, his family was supposedly very rich, and he was probably used to getting his way. But, that did not excuse his inconsiderate behavior or explain the strange vibe I felt whenever I was around him.

I turned to Emma. "Do you believe we can sense the vibrations of other people?"

Emma raised an eyebrow, as if to say, "No, that's crazy," but instead she said, "What do you mean?"

"You know, like their vibrations. Like, do you believe that you can sense what someone's true intent or motivations are just by sensing the vibrations they give off?"

Emma chuckled. "That assumes people actually emit vibrations. Other than the vibrations of their

101

beating heart or their digesting intestines, I don't think people give off vibrations."

I frowned. "What about how they say dogs can sense fear? You know, like that. Do you think people can sense fear or other emotions?"

"I can tell you are serious, but I'd have to see it proven by science. Otherwise, I just don't believe it," said Emma. "Sorry."

I watched as Clayton walked back and forth, looking down into the ocean. It looked like he was taking notes, but I couldn't tell for sure. Maybe he was just holding a small rock.

"Well, I think we can sense vibrations, and I don't like Clayton's."

"He can be a bit … abrupt," Emma agreed. "But, I think he is basically an okay person. He just grew up rich in the City. That probably explains why he doesn't act exactly like we country villagers do."

I doubted that very much, but I could tell my conversation with Emma was at a dead end. I noticed that Clayton was done with his observations, and he had started walking back in the direction of the village.

Day 17 – Afternoon

With the exception of Clayton's suspicious behavior, yesterday had been a good day. We made nearly three hundred emeralds.

On my way home, I had passed Biff's SUP School and Pool. He claimed that he had made fifty emeralds. I did not know if he was telling the truth, but I really didn't care. As long as Emma and I kept making emeralds, I didn't mind if Biff did too. Maybe he'd stop being such a bully if he had some money to help his self-esteem.

This morning was uneventful.

Emma and I surfed and then opened the beach to our customers. The emeralds were pouring in. I taught a few villager kids how to surf. Sales at the snack shack were almost continuous. A couple dozen villagers were in the water surfing.

Yes, sir. Things were going great.

I sat in a chair, getting a tan and looking out at the happy tourists and local villagers enjoying my wave.

They looked like floating emeralds, which, in a way, they were since they had to pay to use my wave.

I felt a swell of greed rising within me. I fought against it. It was okay to make money, but not to be so greedy that you could think of nothing else. The greed was a villager curse. That is what had led me to nearly fight Biff the other day over two measly emeralds. I needed to keep that greed in check. I needed to remember how lucky I was.

The swell of greed was gone. I felt the warm sun on my body. I smelled the salt air drifting in from the breaking waves. I heard the laughter of everyone playing in the ocean.

What could go wrong? I thought as I put my arms behind my head and exhaled a long, calming breath.

That was when I heard the scream.

I jumped up from my chair and put my hand to my forehead, blocking the sunlight from my eyes so that I could see better. I scanned the ocean, but saw nothing.

Emma rushed to my side. "What was that?" she asked in a panicked voice.

I shook my head. "I'm not sure. A scream from the water, but I can't see anything."

Another scream.

A young villager raced up to us. "A squid is attacking my brother."

"What?" Emma and I said in unison. "But squids are passive mobs."

"Save my brother," said the villager, pointing at the water. "He's over there!"

"Turn off the waves," I shouted to Emma as I grabbed my SUP and paddled out as quickly as I could.

I scanned the water, looking for any sign of the squid and villager. I saw nothing. Then, I noticed a surfboard floating in the water. I stroked over to it quickly.

I could not see anything. Until ... I looked down.

I saw a squid dragging a young villager down into the depths of the ocean. I had to act fast. I dove off the SUP and swam down to the squid. I looked at the young villager. He was struggling to get free. I pulled at the squid's tentacles, but that only made it tighten its grip on the villager.

I swam next to the squid and punched it in the head. This made the squid loosen its grip on the villager, and he was able to escape and swim to the surface.

I was following him to the surface when I was enveloped by a cloud of black ink. I couldn't see anything. I became disoriented.

Was I swimming up or down?

Then, I felt a tentacle grab my leg and pull me down. I kicked at the tentacle but its grip tightened. I struggled against it, but I could not free myself. I was being pulled deeper and deeper.

I could feel my health decreasing.

Was this really it? Killed by a squid? How embarrassing.

At least I had saved the young villager. That had to count for something.

I had given up hope and was contemplating where I would like to respawn – Capitol City, maybe – when I suddenly felt the tentacle release its grip. I was able to see through the murky water that the squid was flashing red.

Something had killed it! I hoped it had not been a bigger squid!

Then, I felt an arm grab me and pull me to the surface.

As I broke the surface of the water, I coughed and spit water from my lungs. I saw stars as I felt two hands put me on top of my SUP. The hands held me on the board as I coughed some more, before finally regaining something like a normal breathing rhythm.

I looked around and saw Claire was holding me on the board. Behind her, standing on his SUP was ... Biff?

"Thanks, guys," I said, completely surprised.

Claire smiled reassuringly. "We heard the screams and paddled over to investigate. We saw you save that young villager and then not resurface. It was scary." Claire shivered as she finished speaking.

I looked at Biff. "Yeah, it was intense. I think you are a dork and a loser, but I don't want you to die," he said.

"Thanks, Biff, that means a lot coming from you." (I don't know why I said that. Maybe it was the euphoria of still being alive. My brain was clearly not functioning properly.)

"Biff dove in and stabbed the squid with his sword, and I followed and carried you to the surface," said Claire. "My parents aren't going to believe this when I tell them."

I smiled weakly. "Can you paddle me to shore? I don't feel like being in the ocean anymore today."

"Sure. Just sit there on the front part of the SUP," said Claire as she stood up and started to paddle.

As we got closer to the shore, I could see Emma's face. She was relieved I was alive. She rushed into the shallows of the water and pulled me from the board onto the shore. Someone must have told my parents what had happened because they were there too.

"My baby," shouted my mom as she hugged me close.

How embarrassing, but reassuring at the same time.

My dad moved in and we had a group hug.

Still embarrassing, but I wasn't pushing them away.

Finally, we ended the hug, and I looked around and said, "That was crazy. I've never heard of a squid attacking anyone before. Aren't they normally docile?"

Everyone nodded. No one said anything, but I noticed Biff looked uncomfortable, like he wanted to say something, but just couldn't bring himself to utter the words.

"What is it, Biff?" I asked.

Biff rubbed his over-sized head with his meaty, bully hands and said, "Well, it's just that ... right before I stabbed the squid, I saw its eyes."

Biff shivered. His words stopped. I could tell it was something intense. Finally, Biff managed the strength to continue.

"Its eyes. Its evil eyes. They were ... glowing red."

Before I could ask a follow up question, two village police officers rushed over to us.

"We heard that a squid attacked and nearly killed a young villager," said one of them. "Is that true?"

We all nodded.

"In that case, I'm shutting this surf park thingy down until we can make sure this won't happen again."

"What?!?" I shouted. "You can't do that! This was just a freak occurrence. Squids are normally docile. You can't shut down my wave, bro."

The officer walked over and loomed above me. He was imposing and authoritative. *Was he going to arrest me?*

"Look, kid, first of all, I'm not your bro. Second of all, I don't care what you think you know about the behavioral imperatives of squids. A kid almost drowned here, and we aren't letting anyone in the water until we think it is safe. Got it?" He finished by jabbing a finger a few inches in front of my face.

I sighed. My shoulders slumped. "Yes, sir."

My dream to be a surfer had been crushed. My life was no longer my own. I looked over at Emma. I could tell she was sad too.

I put my hands in my face and sobbed.

END of Book 2

DIARY OF A SURFER VILLAGER

Book 3

(an unofficial Minecraft book)

Day 18

I woke up this morning with a sense of dread.

My sense was correct.

Today, was the worst day of my life.

Let's review: My surf park thingy was closed by the police. I wouldn't be able to make anymore emeralds and, even worse, would not be able to surf the waves Emma and I had created.

And to make matters even more horrible, I had finally decided upon a name for the surf park thingy, but it was closed so no one would ever get to hear it. I had decided to call it "Jimmy and Emma's Surf 'n Snack."

Such a **sick** name!

Although I understood the reasons why the police wanted to close the Surf 'n Snack in order to ensure the safety of all villagers and tourists from squid attacks, I was positive no other squids would ever attack.

I could not shake Biff's account of the squid's glowing red, evil eyes. Obviously, it was not a normal squid. Or, maybe it was a normal squid, but something had been done to it.

Something. Was. Very. Wrong.

As I lay in bed trying to puzzle the mystery of the red-eyed squid, I suddenly had a positive thought. Emma and I had made a few thousand emeralds in a very short period of time. Although we were not rich by the standards of your average greedy Minecraft villager, we were rich for kids our age. Most twelve-year-old villagers only had a few dozen emeralds at best, and most had less.

But, my relative wealth did not make me feel happy. What would I do with the money? The only thing I wanted to do in life was to surf, and now that was gone. I couldn't even move my surf park to another location anywhere near the village because it would be shut down by the police for fear of squid attacks. And, I was too young to move away from home to create a surf park in some other part of the ocean.

Basically, even if I had all the emeralds in the world, they would be useless to solve my problem.

Tear. Sniff.

In order to try to snap myself out of my funk, I decided to go downstairs and eat some breakfast. When I got to the kitchen, I saw that my mom had prepared my most favorite food of all time: apple pie.

My mom came over and gave me a hug and said, "I'm glad you survived that squid attack yesterday."

I shrugged, pretending like I was dominant and unafraid. "Yeah, it's cool. But now I can't go surfing anymore."

My mom held onto my shoulders and pushed me away to arm's length and looked me in the eyes with a very serious expression. "I don't want you to go surfing, or swimming, or any of that other nonsense you do in the ocean. The water is dangerous. You need to stay out of it."

I suddenly became upset. "I'll never stay out of the ocean. Surfing is too awesome. But, it doesn't matter right now. The police won't let me go in."

My mom shook her head sadly and said, "Sit down, Jimmy. Eat one of these apple pies. You'll feel better."

I quickly devoured one of the apple pies. The sugary sweet baked fruit did make me feel better, but only for a brief moment. This must be how people feel who need to eat to be happy. It only lasts for a short moment and then you need to eat more.

I looked into the living room and saw my dad sitting in a chair reviewing his business account books. "What are you doing, Dad?"

"Just adding up the emeralds we made this month at our store. It was a pretty good month," he said, grinning, a greedy glint appearing in his eyes.

I sighed. "I wish I could say the same. Emma and I were doing very well but now are making nothing. It's not fair that something I don't have any control over destroys my business."

My dad looked at me and smiled knowingly. "Jimmy, there are many things we can control in this life, but we cannot control everything. You had a great business going there and this is just a setback.

115

Eventually, the police will let you go back in the ocean and you can reopen for business. It might take a few weeks or months, but you'll be back."

I wanted to believe my dad, but I thought he was lying to me. I was sure this was the end of my business world. Now, I would just be a poor villager who would be forced to inherit the family business instead of creating something of my own to be proud of.

"I doubt it, Dad," I said, an angry edge in my voice.

My father shook his head. "You know, back when you are very little, a giant zombie and husk horde encircled the village of Zombie Bane. It took weeks before the players could come clear them out. Most zombies would die in the fire of daylight, but the husks remained. Then, when night fell, the zombies would respawn. It was horrible. But your mom and I had saved up enough emeralds and enough food that we were able to make it through. Sure, we lost a solid month's worth of income, but these things happen. Trust me, you'll get back on your feet one of these days."

I shrugged in response. I didn't want to admit that my dad's story made a lot of sense and he actually kind of cheered me up. I just wasn't ready to be happy yet.

I stood up. "Yeah, I guess. Whatever. I'm gonna go back to my room."

I walked upstairs and went into my room and pulled out my surf magazine. I looked at the beautiful pictures of waves and tubes in exotic locations and I started to cry.

Day 19 – Morning

I slept until the rays of the sun poured through my window, hitting me in the face, and forcing me to wake up. It was about nine o'clock in the morning.

A few days ago, I would have already been making tons of emeralds. But now, I was just another twelve-year-old sleeping in and wasting the day.

Who cares, I thought. I guess that's what my life has come to. Just a waste of time.

At that moment, I decided to spend the entire day in bed. I would only get up to use the bathroom or eat a few snacks. I wasn't going to get out of my pajamas. I didn't care that they smelled.

About 30 minutes later, there was a knock on my door.

"What is it?" I asked, upset that someone had dared to disturb my pathetic-ness.

The door cracked open. It was my mom. "Emma is here. She wants to talk to you."

I shrugged. "Send her up."

My mom laughed. "I'm not going to send her up here to this disgusting pigsty. It smells horrible. Open a window, put on some clean clothes, and come downstairs."

I didn't want to put on any clean clothes, but I also didn't want to be too gross around my friends. I walked over to my closet and picked out a super awesome – jk lol – brown robe. No multicolored robes for me. Just pathetic brown robes. I looked just like everybody else.

After I put on my robe, I quickly brushed my teeth and tossed a handful of water in my hair so it wouldn't look so greasy. I left my room and went downstairs where I found Emma sitting at the kitchen table eating a slice of apple pie.

"This apple pie is awesome," she said with her mouth full, crumbs of crust falling from her lips. "Your mom is a great baker."

I shrugged. "Yeah, hurr, I guess she's pretty good. I had apple pie for breakfast yesterday."

Emma's eyes widened with shock and jealousy. "I wish my mom would let me eat apple pie for breakfast," she said as she stuffed another piece of pie in her mouth.

"She only gives me pie in the morning when I'm depressed. It's not that great."

Emma laughed. "Stop being such a derp. Let's do something."

I sighed. "Why? We can't surf any waves. The cops have the ocean closed."

Emma rolled her eyes and shook her head. "The ocean's pretty big, in case you forgot. We can SUP wherever we want. Besides, even if there are more evil killer squids out there, we can see them from on top of our SUPs and get away from them."

I laughed so hard I almost snorted out a booger, but recovered in time to prevent embarrassment. "There aren't any more evil squids. Biff said it looked evil. It was probably possessed or something. There's no way it was natural. I bet nothing like that will ever happen again. The police are just being stupid for shutting down the Surf 'n Snack."

Emma thought about it for a minute. She pursed her lips and crinkled her eyes in thought. "Yeah, hurr, maybe you're right. But, there's nothing we can do about that right now. So let's go have some fun. Maybe we can even spend a few of those emeralds we made."

I had to admit, getting outside and getting a little sun and exercise did sound like a good idea. I didn't want to admit it, but Emma was right. Plus, it would be fun to spend some of the emeralds we made. Maybe we could buy some action figures or a few good Minecraft diaries. I guess it might be fun.

"Okay, sounds a good idea. Let me go get my swim trunks on and we can grab our SUPs and go down to the ocean. But, I'll have to be careful. My mom doesn't want me playing in the ocean, so I need to sneak the SUP out."

Emma smiled and nodded her understanding. "Great. I'm just going to have another piece of this apple pie while you get ready."

After I changed – my bathing suit hidden under my robe – I walked back downstairs and Emma and I went to the side of my house where I grabbed my SUP and paddle.

We then walked to Emma's house. But, instead of going straight for her SUP, she told me to come check out her latest invention. I put down my board and followed her.

When we got to the side yard of her house, there was a big pile of something that looked like a lot of ropes tied together. "See, I made a net," said Emma proudly.

I scratched the bristles of my blonde hair, confused. "What, are you going fishing or something?"

Emma slapped her forehead. "No, silly, it's a protective net. We can put it around our surf area and it will keep out any squids that happen to drift in our direction."

My eyes got wide with understanding. "Do you think that will work?"

"Yes, I'm sure it will. I just need to convince the police it will be strong enough to keep out any squids. I think if they observe it for a while they'll see that squids can't get through and maybe they'll let us reopen the Surf 'n Snack."

I rushed over to Emma and gave her a hug. (I know, I know. It's always the girls who do the hugging, but not this time. Not this time.)

Day 19 – Afternoon

Emma and I had been paddling around in silence for about half an hour. A few other kids and looked at us from the shore and shouted that we should come in to avoid the evil squid. We just ignored them.

I couldn't believe there were no police officers around. They just shut down my business and don't bother to guard it???

I stroked over closer to Emma and asked, "What do you think caused the squid to have the evil red eyes that Biff noticed?"

Emma shook her head and shrugged. "I've never heard of such a thing. I've been trying to think of some sort of scientific explanation for what may have turned the squid's eyes red and made it act the way it did. The only thing I can come up with is that maybe it was sick."

I thought back to the incident as I was being dragged down to the depths and had believed that I was about to lose the last of my air bubbles and die flashing red and then evaporating in a puff of smoke, if smoke could exist under the water.

As I relived that horrific moment, I shuddered. I seemed to recall feeling an evil vibration coming from the squid. Although I had not seen its eyes, I distinctly remembered the feeling of evil and dread coming over me.

"You know something, Emma, hurr, as I was being dragged down to the bottom of the ocean by the squid, I felt something strange. I felt as though the squid were truly evil."

Emma chuckled. "That makes no scientific sense. Squids are passive mobs. I don't think a squid can be evil or good. It just exists."

I shook my head as I continued to paddle along next to her. "I know, but I really did feel something evil from it. Like maybe it was possessed or poisoned or something. Do you think there's a potion that could do that?"

Emma contemplated my question for a moment. I could tell she was accessing the database of her mind. After about 10 seconds, she shook her head. "No, I don't think there's any potion that can do that."

I reached up and rubbed my chin in thought. "What about an Evoker? Do you think one could have cast a spell or conjured some sort of evilness to make the squid do what it did?"

Again, Emma paused for an extended period of time to think. "I really don't know. I'm unsure what Evokers are actually fully capable of. We may need to do some research."

"Research? Where can we do that?"

Emma looked at me like I was the biggest idiot in the world. "Um, the library? A bookstore?"

I smiled sheepishly and said, "Oh, yeah, of course. Let's get to shore, dry off and go see about that research."

Day 19 – Late Afternoon

After Emma and I had dropped off our SUP boards and had changed into normal brown villager robes, we went to the town library.

The inside of the library looked like you might expect it to look. There were stacks of books on shelves everywhere. It smelled like leather and slightly damp dog due to all the old pages of paper and parchment. I'd only been in there once or twice, usually just with my parents. Libraries and I didn't get along.

As we walked through the front door I saw the scariest looking librarian I had seen in a long time.

Well, since I'd only really seen one or two librarians in the past and that was like five years ago, maybe it was the same librarian. I don't know. Anyway, the librarian was very scary.

"I don't like the looks of that guy," I whispered to Emma.

Emma laughed. "Librarians are harmless. And besides, that's a woman."

"Really?"

Emma nodded and slapped the side of my shoulder with the back of her hand indicating for me to follow her to the librarian. We walked up to "her" and Emma talked.

"We are looking for books discussing Evokers and the sorts of magic they can do."

A look of shock and dismay disfigured the librarian's face. She put her hand to her chest and fluttered it like a fan as if to indicate that she was having heart palpitations. Then she spoke in a creaky cracky old lady voice, "We don't have filth like that in our library."

"Filth?" said Emma, surprised. "Come on, lady. We just want to do some scientific research."

The librarian moved her fluttering hand from her chest to her face, as if fanning herself with it would somehow cleanse her of the horrible things she had just heard emanate from Emma's mouth.

"Well, I don't know anything about 'scientific research,' but I can assure you, young lady, we don't have any books about Evokers, or magic, or witches, or any of that stuff."

"What about zombie books?" I asked.

The librarian looked at me like I was daft. "Of course we have zombie books! This is Zombie Bane after all. Zombies are totally different," she explained, her hand still fluttering in front of her face.

"Well, then, where can we find books with information about that filth?" asked Emma.

This time, the librarian lifted her other hand up to her face and fluttered both of them in front of her as rapidly as she could. "Well, I'm sure that old weirdo Mr. Blaze has some of those sorts of books in his disgusting bookstore."

"Thanks for the information," said Emma with a smile, saluting the librarian by quickly tapping two fingers against her forehead.

When the librarian had realized that she had just told two twelve-year-old villagers where to find such horrific filth, she passed out.

Even though she had been mean to us, we couldn't ignore a possible medical emergency. We ran around the librarian's desk and lifted her up and put her on a chair. Then, doing what seemed like the most obvious thing to do, we fanned her face with our hands.

Apparently four hands work better than two because she regained consciousness rather quickly and said, "Thank you, children, but don't go to that bookstore. You'll regret it."

Emma and I shrugged, said "You're welcome," and left the library to go over to Mr. Blaze's bookstore.

As we left the library, my stomach grumbled. "Hey, Emma, hurr, let's get something to eat at the Junction before we go to the bookstore. I'm starving."

"Cool," said Emma.

The Zombie Junction Snack Shack – or, "the Junction," as the locals called it – was owned by a family that lived a block away from my house. The kids were older than me, so I didn't really know them very well. But all the locals agreed they made the best food. Some of the other restaurants were more popular with tourists, but people in the know went to the Junction for their eats.

Emma and I sat down at a table near a window so we could watch tourists walking by.

"I can't believe school starts in a couple weeks and I can't go surfing," I sighed, feeling sorry for myself.

"I'm excited for school to start," said Emma. "I heard the sixth grade teacher is a whiz when it comes to science."

"Ugh, I hate science."

Emma shook her head. "But look at what science has done for you. It created the Surf 'n Snack. Without science, you'd still be daydreaming and staring at surf magazines."

I shrugged. "I suppose."

Just then, the waiter came over and asked us what we wanted. Emma ordered three apple pies and a glass of milk. I ordered a watermelon, a carrot salad, roast mutton, and a glass of water.

The waiter smiled as he wrote down the order and raised a questioning eyebrow, probably thinking it was bizarre that one person at the table was ordering all desserts and the other person was ordering a full dinner and it was only 3 o'clock in the afternoon. But, like a good waiter, he didn't question the food choices, he just took the order and went away.

I stared out the window watching tourists excitedly pointing at different landmarks. The Junction was only a few doors down from one of the locations where my great great gramps had killed one of his ten zombies. I think it was zombie number eight or maybe number six; I just couldn't remember.

"Sometimes I wish we lived in a town that didn't have a beach," I said. "At least then, I wouldn't want to go surfing."

Emma rolled her eyes. "Really? What about all these landlocked tourists who come here and paid to take surf lessons from you? Maybe you *would* want to go surfing."

As usual, Emma was right. I didn't want to talk about it anymore.

A moment later, the waiter arrived with our food and we ate in silence. When we were done, I left five emeralds on the table to pay for the meal, including a one emerald tip for the waiter.

Mr. Blaze's bookstore was only about a five minute walk from the Junction. The outside looked like any other storefront in the village of Zombie Bane. Blocks stacked high, a sturdy door, and a window to show off the items for sale inside.

We open the door and walked in. It seemed like any other bookstore I'd been inside. Not that I'd been in very many. Books everywhere. The latest bestsellers. I saw several copies of one of my favorite books, *Baby Zeke: The Diary of a Chicken Jockey*, displayed on an end cap. There were also some biographies, the most prominent of which was the book written by my father about my grandfather. In case you forgot it's called *Cornelius: Bane of Zombies*. There were probably about 100 copies of it stacked in the form of a pyramid located on a table just as you entered the bookstore. The books confronted you and almost demanded you purchase one of them.

There were a few tourists milling about browsing the books. A couple of them were caring copies of *Cornelius: Bane of Zombies*, and the rest just had a random assortment of entertaining fiction and some guidebooks.

We walked up to the information counter and I asked, "Is Mr. Blaze around?"

The teenager behind the counter slowly looked up and said, "Hey, are you the kids who run the surf school thingy?"

I nodded. "The Surf 'n Snack," I explained while pointing at Emma. "She built the thing."

He looked over at Emma and nodded approvingly. "Nice work. Too bad about that stupid squid. I was thinking about coming over for a surf lesson myself one of these days."

I sighed. "Yeah, anyway, that's kind of why we want to talk to Mr. Blaze. We were hoping to ask him a few questions."

The teenager behind the cash register glanced to the far corner of the bookstore where there was a small door. He pointed at the door and said, "He's in there. Doing inventory or something. Just go up to the door and knock. He'll open it. You can tell him what you want."

We thanked the teenager and walked over to the corner. Before we knocked on the door, I said to Emma, "So, how are we to broach the subject with this guy? Just asking for all his occult books?"

Emma shrugged. "I don't think we are looking for occult books. I think we are looking for research about Evokers. That's different. We don't want to *become* Evokers, just learn about them."

I nodded. "I guess so. Maybe you should do the talking."

Emma smiled. "I was going to anyway."

We walked up to the door and I knocked. After a few seconds there was no response and so I knocked again. At that point the door latch clicked and the door creaked open.

Standing in front of us was a fairly normal looking villager, though maybe a little shorter than average. He was wearing a brown robe with a few stains on it, probably from food or maybe some soup he had spilled on himself. His hair was a little greasy, like he hadn't taken a shower in a week or two, but he didn't smell. He was wearing thick red [?!?] glasses, probably having ruined his eyes from reading too much in low light. The glasses had slid down his nose a little bit and he pushed them back before he said, "Yes? How can I help you?"

Emma looked at him and said, "We were hoping to find some information. Some historical information. Some information about what Evokers are capable of."

Mr. Blaze looked a little surprised by the question but, unlike the librarian, he was not shocked. He tilted his head toward the ceiling and looked at the old wooden ceiling tiles. His eyes darted back and forth as he thought about Emma's request. Then he smacked his lips together and looked back down at us and said, "I have some books about Evokers. But, what exactly do you want to know?"

"Well," said Emma, "we want to know if they can possess mobs using their magic. We have a theory and we wanted to see if it was even possible before we explored it further."

Mr. Blaze squinted his eyes together and looked at us. I could tell he had a book that would tell us exactly what we wanted to know but he was assessing us to see if he was going to reveal it to us. Then he asked, "Are you the two kids who run the surf park?"

We nodded.

"Then, hurr, I guess this must be about that squid, right?"

I was surprised he figured it out so quickly. "Yes, you are right. How did you know?"

He shrugged. "I heard a rumor about the squid having evil red eyes. It reminded me of something I read in the book once. In fact, it's the book that I'm going to give to you to help answer your question. Follow me."

Mr. Blaze turned his back to us and led us farther back into the room. We followed him into a smaller adjoining room crammed with books. He motioned for us to shut the door as we entered. I noticed most of the books in the room were just copies of books for sale in the bookstore. But, there was a small cabinet with glass doors that were locked. It was to this cabinet that Mr. Blaze led us.

Mr. Blaze pulled a key out of his pocket and unlocked the cabinet. He reached in and moved his finger slowly across the spines of the books as he read their titles. When he found the one he was looking for, he grabbed the spine and pulled the book from the cabinet. He turned around wordlessly and walked over to a small table and set the book down. He opened the book to a section, flipped through a few pages until he found what he was looking for, and then gestured to us.

We walked over and stood next to him.

"This book explains the magical powers of the Evokers. Most people know that they can summon vexes to attack others, especially players. But there's a lot more they can do. Normally, they don't bother with their additional powers because the vexes alone tend to be enough. However, they are masters of the dark arts. Go ahead and read it."

We walked up to the book and began to read. It said:

The name Evoker comes from the verb to evoke. Evokers typically are able to summon creatures, known as vexes, from nowhere. They simply materialize. What is little-known is that the Evokers are able to summon creatures to any location they wish. Therefore, an Evoker can summon a vex to the inside of a box or a wall, or any other hollow cavity. There are some who further speculate that Evokers can summon the powers of the vex without the body of a vex, thus enabling them to possess others. There are stories of Evokers in the past who, through much trial and error and pain, perfected this talent. Similarly, there are stories of Evokers who tried but failed to perfect this talent, and instead simply killed the victims they attempted to possess. The last known instance of an Evoker possessing a victim occurred more than 200 years ago.

My jaw was hanging slack. I looked over at Emma and said, "This means an Evoker could have possessed that squid!"

Emma tilted her head back and forth considering this. "Maybe. But it says the last known Evoker who could do this lived over 200 years ago. If that's true, then maybe this ability has died, or, at least, the knowledge of how to perform it has died."

I nodded. "Could be, but a power like that is something someone evil would try to revive if they knew it was possible."

"Exactly!" said Mr. Blaze. "When I heard about that squid and his red eyes, I thought right away he was possessed. The only way to prove it would've been to examine the squid itself, but now it's gone. If there is an Evoker out there who can possess mobs, then it's only a matter of time before the Evoker will attempt to possess villagers and maybe even players. This is very dangerous."

"Do you think the Evoker lives in our village?" I asked, my voice trembling.

Mr. Blaze shook his head. "I doubt it. If someone had been trying to master these dark arts, I think someone would have seen it. Practicing evoking skills requires a lot of attempts and surely they would have summoned vexes that would escape and it would have been noticed. To my knowledge, there hasn't been an Evoker in Zombie Bane for at least 100 years."

I sighed. "Thank you for letting us read this book. At least we know that our theory might be correct. But how do we prove it?"

"Without the squid's body, maybe we never will," said Emma. "But in the meanwhile, I need to go back home and work on my net. We should go by the police department tomorrow and see if they will let us reopen our surf park. We can worry about Evoker possession another time."

Day 20

About ten o'clock in the morning, I went over to Emma's house so we could walk to the police station together to check on the status of our surf park. The police had previously told us they needed to ensure that the area was safe for swimming activities before they would allow us to reopen. I had hoped that in the two days the park was closed they would have reached that conclusion.

The police station was on the other side of the village, so it took us about fifteen minutes to walk there. I jealously watched the tourists entering the various shops and restaurants and spending emeralds by the dozens while Emma and I earned nothing.

Stop it, stop it, I thought. *The emeralds are means to an end they are not the end themselves. Stop being such a greedy villager!*

We were passing by the souvenir shop owned by Biff's family. As his SUP school was also closed due to the squid, I saw him inside folding t-shirts.

Biff looked up from his pile of cheaply-made t-shirts and saw me. In the past, we would've given each other the stink eye and Biff would've made some sort of threatening gesture. But now, after the squid incident and Biff having saved my life, we just acknowledged each other's existence. I could tell that our relationship been changed forever. In some ways, I wish it hadn't been. I wish he was still a bully and the squid incident had never happened. But, at least I was alive to have these wishes. Without Biff's quick thinking, I wouldn't be. I owed him a debt I could never repay.

Emma and I arrived at the police station and walked up to the police officer sitting behind the front desk.

"We'd like to speak with the person in charge of the squid monitoring operation by the surf park," said Emma.

The officer looked at us and raised an eyebrow. "You the kids that own the place?"

We nodded.

"Okay. Give me a minute. I'll go find the sergeant in charge of that investigation."

We walked away from the front desk and sat on some chairs in the lobby. I looked around the police station and then elbowed Emma in the ribs gently. "Hey, look at that picture over there." I pointed. "It says it's an Evoker wanted for his illegal conjuring and magical activities."

Emma squinted at the picture. "All those Evokers look the same to me. How could anyone ever tell them apart?"

WANTED!

for illegal conjuring
and magical activities

I shrugged. "I don't know. But, if there's actually an Evoker who is wanted for improper use of magic, maybe he possessed the squid or at least knows something about the squid or maybe there's a group of Evokers who are doing all kinds of illegal things."

Emma nodded her head silently and pursed her lips in thought. After a few seconds she said, "Could be, I suppose. But let's get our surf park reopened first and then we can worry about illegal Evoking and whether it is related to the squid incident."

I stood up and walked over to the poster. According to the narrative printed on it, the Evoker had been using illegal magic in Capitol City and was on the run. There was no indication he was anywhere near Zombie Bane.

At that moment a police officer, who clearly thought he was very important, walked up to us and said, "You the kids here about the squid?"

We stood up and I said, "Yes. Do you think we can reopen our surf park now?"

He shook his head. "Our monitoring has been inconclusive. We cannot assure the safety of bathers."

"What if we install a net? A squid-proof net," suggested Emma.

The officer rubbed his chin in thought. I could hear his whiskers scratching against his fingertips. "Could work. We'd have to see it in action. Do you have it installed yet?"

Emma shook her head. "I should finish it today. Jimmy and I can install it tomorrow and then you can inspect it."

The officer begrudgingly grunted his assent. "Okay. Get that thing installed and we'll look at it. If we are convinced it will stop squids, then we will probably let you open the place."

I smiled for the first time in two days. "Thank you, officer. We will let you know once the net is installed," I said.

We left the police station and walked to Emma's house and into her backyard where she was building the net. I walked over to the unfinished net and inspected it.

"You really think you can get this thing done in a day?" I asked.

"No problem," said Emma confidently. "I already have all the materials I need, and I've got my technique down."

"Do you need me to help you?"

Emma shook her head. "On something like this, I prefer to work alone. Be back here tomorrow morning and we will load the net into my parents' horse cart and get it over to the surf park."

"Sounds like a great idea. See you tomorrow," I said waving at Emma as I walked away.

Day 21

I woke up early and sprung out of bed. Seriously, I *sprung* out of bed like a *spring*. I was so excited about installing the net and the possibility that we could reopen the surf park soon, that I had a spring in my step.

I'm not sure why people use that metaphor about springs when they are happy or excited. It seems a bit peculiar to me. Most springs are weight-bearing springs. They are not explosive activity springs. So, I'm just not quite sure where the metaphor comes from. Maybe it relates to rabbits hopping and people thinking they looked like a spring when they hopped? I don't know. All that I know is that the saying applied to me this morning.

I got dressed quickly, raced downstairs, and wolfed down a big breakfast that my mom had cooked for me.

There's another metaphor that I think is a little weird. Eating like a wolf. I've never actually watched wolves eat, but I think they normally eat in packs, with the most important wolf eating first and the rest of the wolves sitting around waiting for their turns.

I suppose wolves probably do eat rather quickly because typically a wolf kills an animal and then immediately eats it. I guess you wouldn't want the animal's carcass sitting there too long. Plus, once an animal is killed in Minecraft, it flashes red and turns into a puff of smoke pretty quickly, so if you're a wolf you have to eat the animal very fast before it disappears.

So, I'd have to say that I did, in fact, *wolf down* my breakfast.

After eating, I rushed out of the house and went to Emma's.

When I arrived, Emma was already loading the finished net into the back of the horse cart. I jogged over and helped her lift the net. It was very heavy.

"Wow, Emma, this thing is massive!"

She nodded as she grunted with exertion. "Yeah, it is. But we have to span the entire stretch of ocean from shore to shore in order to keep the squids out. It's a good thing that our surf park is in an alcove so we only have to close off one side and not both sides."

I continued to shove the net into the back of a horse cart. "Yeah, that was fortuitous."

Emma looked at me and raised an eyebrow quizzically. "I didn't know you knew what fortuitous meant."

I shrugged. "Sometimes I surprise myself."

When we finished loading the net into the back of the horse cart, we hitched Emma's horse to the cart and hopped in the two seats at the front. Emma grabbed the reins and snapped them. The horse began to move and pulled the cart at a slow, meandering pace.

It took us about thirty minutes to get from Emma's house to the surf park area where we could begin installing the net. As we were preparing the net anchors on one side of the shore, Biff and his cousin Claire showed up.

I looked at them suspiciously. "What are you guys doing here?"

Biff shuffled his feet uncomfortably and scratched his hair nervously. Claire just smiled. Biff began to explain. "Well, my parents have a friend at the police station and they said something about you guys installing a net today. And, hurr, I was wondering if you might install it to protect my SUP area too?"

I sighed. He had saved my life....

I looked over at Emma. "Is it big enough for that?"

Emma thought for a few moments and then said, "It's probably pretty close. I may need to make it a few more blocks wide to cover the opening by Biff's SUP school. But, it would probably work."

I looked over at Biff. "Look, since you saved my life I'm willing to move the net farther over. But, if we need to use any more material to enlarge the net, you have to pay for it. Deal?"

Biff smiled the biggest smile I've ever seen anyone smile during my entire life. "No problem. I'll even pay for half the net. I just want to be able to reopen my school too."

Biff offering to pay for something that he didn't have to? What is going on?

"Help us load the net back into the horse cart and we will drive it down towards your school so that we can anchor it to the shore there," said Emma. Biff rushed over and began loading the net with Emma.

I was about to start helping too when Claire walked up to me and handed me a present.

"Here. I got this for you."

I could feel my cheeks blushing. It was so embarrassing. "Um, thanks. Hurr, uh, what is this for?"

Claire shrugged. "I just thought you'd like it. I had fun in Zombie Bane this summer and I wanted to give you something."

That didn't seem like much of an explanation to me, but whatever. It was a present. I tore the paper off the present and lifted the lid from the box. Inside was a multicolored robe! I pulled the robe out and held it up. "Oh my Notch, this is awesome! Thank you so much!"

Claire smiled. "Sure. You'll be the coolest dressed kid in all of Zombie Bane."

I turned around and showed it to Emma. "Emma! Look at what Claire gave me!"

Emma cast a cool glance at the robe and then at Claire. I could almost see the icicles shooting from Emma's eyes and hitting Claire. "Yes. Very nice," said Emma in an extremely slow, vicious voice.

What has gotten into her?!?

I shuddered and turned around to look at Claire. "Anyway, thanks. I'll probably save it to wear for the first day of school."

"That sounds like a great idea," said Claire as she stepped closer to me and gave me a hug.

Again with the hugging? I just didn't get it.

When Claire stopped hugging me and backed away I asked, "Hey, where's your brother Clayton?"

"Oh, father summoned him home quickly for some reason a few days ago. I'm not exactly sure why, but he is the next in line to succeed in the family business, so it probably has something to do with some important business deal."

I nodded. "Well, I had better put this robe back into the box so it doesn't get dirty. Then, we can help Emma and Biff install the net."

Claire giggled. "Silly. I'm not going to help install the net. I don't know how to do that kind of stuff. I'll see you guys later."

Claire began walking back to the village. I waved good-bye to her and went to help install the net.

Once Emma, Biff, and I had the net loaded in the horse cart, we drove down the beach a little ways and found a good location to anchor the net on the other side of Biff's SUP school. After attaching one side to the anchors, we stretched it out toward the other side of the shore.

Fortunately, the net was wide enough to reach the other side, but we had to add some additional netting at the bottom of the net so it could reach the bottom of the ocean. We took turns diving down and anchoring the extended net to the bottom of the ocean.

After we had connected all points of the net, we stood on the shore and watched as some squids attempted to swim past the net but simply bounced off and were redirected the other way. The holes in the net were big enough for smaller fish to swim through, but not something as large as a squid.

"Looks like it's working," said Emma, a grin spreading across her face.

I put my hand up for a high five from Emma, but she just ignored me. "Dang, don't leave me hanging like that."

"I thought maybe you were too cool for me with your new multicolored robe," said Emma sarcastically.

"Come on, it was a gift. I didn't ask for it." I said.

"Whatever," said Emma, folding her arms across her chest.

Biff was oblivious to our dispute. He was staring in amazement at the net. Then he said, his voice cracking and a tear rolling down his cheek, "You guys are awesome. Let's go tell the police we got the net installed and they can come look at tomorrow."

We all agreed and started walking toward the horse cart.

Day 22 – Morning

The police had agreed to show up and inspect the net at 10 o'clock in the morning today. Emma, Biff, and I arrived at 9:30 to make sure everything was still in place. It was. The net was extremely secure. We pulled at it with all our might, but it didn't budge.

When the police arrived, we explained to them how the net was anchored to both sides of the ocean and all the way to the bottom. We told them how we had watched and no squids could get past. Thus, we said, both of our schools and surfing areas were safe.

The police, of course, didn't believe us and had to confirm everything we had just told them. The officers got in a boat and inspected both sides of the net to ensure it truly was anchored properly. They then sent a diver down to inspect the anchorage points at the bottom of the ocean.

After about an hour, the police agreed that the net was completely secure.

The police then patrolled up and down the ocean to ensure there were no squids on the school side of the net. They found only one and killed it. Once that was done, they told us we had a clean bill of health and we could open our surf school that afternoon!

I was so happy, I sank down to my knees, threw my arms to the heavens, shouted, "Praise Be to Notch!" and wept tears of joy.

The police officers looked at me like I was in need of serious help and walked off.

Day 22 – Afternoon

At noon, I watched as Emma turned on the switch to the wave machine to make sure it still worked. It did.

Emma and I paddled out and caught a few. I got super barreled on the left and Emma was carving a right. I almost didn't want to open the Surf 'n Snack today. I just wanted to have it to myself. But, I needed to make as much money as I could while summer was still in full swing and tourists were all over the town.

We each caught a few more waves and then decided we needed to open the park to everybody else.

Emma ran to her house, got on her horse, and rode around the streets of the village announcing the reopening of the Surf 'n Snack as well as Biff's SUP school. Within an hour we had a huge crowd on hand and had made 150 emeralds.

Hurr. Sweet relief!

Day 23 – Morning

Today, I arrived at the Surf 'n Snack at 7:30 in the morning. All villager kids had to start school in a few weeks, and so did most of the tourist villagers. Emma and I agreed to have the surf park open from 8:00 in the morning until sunset every day until school started.

We – or should I say, "I" – wanted to make as much money as possible during the final days of summer.

When Emma and I opened the surf park at 8:00 o'clock there was already a line of fifty people waiting to surf. We got them all through the gate and into the water fairly quickly. Once the initial press of customers was processed, I relaxed a bit looked out at the waves. They had a calming effect on me.

I had been staring at the waves for about five minutes when I heard a familiar voice say, "Hey dude, what's up?"

I looked over and saw Laird. "Laird! How's it going? Have you been accumulating lots of awesome stuff in Minecraft?"

"Sure. I've got a complete suit of diamond armor and a diamond sword now. It's all getting pretty easy."

"Maybe you should go over to the hard-core area of the world and see how well you do there?" I suggested with a wink.

Laird shivered with fear. "No way. The hard-core part of Minecraft is too crazy for me. Besides, there's no waves over there." Laird smiled.

I smiled back.

Laird handed me a couple emeralds and went over and picked out a surfboard. When he came back he said, "By the way, have you heard about the new wave pool that just opened up in Capitol City?"

My blood turned to ice. I felt nauseous. My mouth went dry. "What wave pool?"

"Yeah, it's called the Dretsky Wave Pool and SUP Center. It's inside some giant building."

"Dretsky?" I said. "Did you say 'Dretsky'?"

Laird nodded. "Yeah. I guess they are some sort of big important family in Capitol City. I've heard the wave pool is pretty rad. You should check it out." And with that, Laird ran into the water and began surfing.

I sat there as rage flooded my body. Clayton Dretsky, Biff's cousin and Claire's brother, had stolen my idea and stolen Emma's technology. That's why he was lurking around on the other side of the shore that one day. I couldn't believe this.

Just then Claire and Biff walked up.

"I want to rent a surfboard," said Claire. "I'm going home tomorrow and want to catch a few more waves."

I exploded with anger. "Why would you want to do that? Why don't you just surf in your family's wave pool? You're such horrible people!"

Claire stared at me like a shocked llama seeing a wolf for the first time. "What are you talking about?"

"Like you don't know. Your brother started a wave pool. He stole my idea and now he's going to steal all my money by attracting tourists to Capitol City to use it."

"I don't know what you are talking about," insisted Claire.

"Yeah, what are you talking about?" asked Biff, confused.

"Laird just told me that the Dretsky Wave Pool and SUP Center just opened in Capitol City."

"SUP center?" gasped Biff.

"Yeah, they stole my idea and now they are going to steal both of our businesses."

Emma had apparently overheard all this and walked up. "That's pretty low for Clayton to steal from us, but we will still get business. Tourists are still going to come to Zombie Bane."

"Yeah, but this was my idea. This is industrial espionage. Clayton can't get away with this." I turned my wrath on Claire. "Claire, I'm not going to rent you a surfboard. I don't know if you were involved in this or not, but I don't like your family anymore."

"I can't believe you said that to me. Didn't I just give you a multicolored robe yesterday?" said Claire in shock.

I laughed. "You think you can buy me? Take your robe back then." I was being super vicious.

I could see the tears forming in Claire's eyes. "I just wanted to do something nice for you. You seem like a nice guy."

I laughed. "Whatever. Get out here."

(I was being a total jerk. Inside, I knew Claire probably did not deserve to be treated like this, but I was so angry, my judgment was gone.)

Claire stared at me, tears forming in her eyes. Then her eyes got hard and she stared at me. Her stare was like nails. And, truth be told, it made me feel somewhat uncomfortable. She then turned and walked away without another word.

Biff watched his cousin walk away and then said to me, "Dude, I'm upset too, but that was pretty harsh."

"I don't care. I've had the most technologically advanced amazing idea in the history of Minecraft and now that idiot from Capitol City steals it from me? I'm not gonna take this lying down."

"What are you gonna do, then? You are already standing up," Emma said in a terrible attempt at humor.

I didn't say anything because, well, I had no idea what to do. Instead, I grabbed a surfboard and paddled out to sit next to Laird.

"Laird, any chance you are going to Capitol City soon?" I asked.

"Yeah, I was thinking about heading there tomorrow. I want to check out the wave pool. I heard it has three different waves."

I slapped my forehead. This was worse than I had imagined. "Three different waves?"

"Yeah, I heard they've got a big barrel, a long point break, and a mushy little beach break for the beginners to practice on. Sounds v. awesome."

Actually, it did not sound awesome, v. or otherwise. It sounded like I was going to be put out of business.

"Sure, it does. Hurr, anyway, I'd like to check it out too. You think I could come with you?"

Laird shrugged. "Sure, if it's okay with your parents."

"I'm sure it will be."

"Okay, well if it's okay with your parents, meet me over at the hotel at 9:00 in the morning tomorrow. That's when I plan to leave," said Laird as he paddled for a wave.

"Okay, I will," I shouted just as Laird stood up on the wave and began to ride to shore.

Laird looked back, threw me a shaka, and said, "Cool dude." And then disappeared into the barrel.

Day 23 – Evening

After we closed the Surf 'n Snack for the day, we counted our several hundred emeralds of earnings for the day, and Emma and I parted ways and went home.

Emma knew I wanted to go to Capitol City and she was thinking about whether she should go too. I told her she needed to stay here and run the surf park. And she agreed. Reluctantly.

When I got home, my mom had a delicious dinner waiting for me. There was sliced watermelon, mushroom stew, cookies, pork chops, steaks, and steamed carrots. I sat down but didn't eat because I didn't have much of an appetite.

"Aren't you hungry?" asked my mom. "You've been working all day."

I pushed some food around my plate with a fork. "I just heard that Clayton Dretsky opened up a wave pool in Capitol City. He stole my idea."

"That's unfortunate," said my dad. "At least there's enough surfers to go around."

I dropped my fork. "Are you even upset? He stole my idea!"

"Well, he did copy your idea. But ideas are a dime a dozen. It's the execution of the idea that matters. If he stole your wave-making technology, that would be different."

"That's what I'm trying to say. I'm sure he did. He was lurking around our wave maker about a week ago and now he suddenly has a wave pool?"

My mom nodded her head. "It would seem as though maybe he did steal your technology. That's illegal."

"Exactly," I said with a determined voice. "That's why I'm going to Capitol City tomorrow to confront him."

My parents both laughed. "You are not going to Capitol City tomorrow. You have to stay here and run your business."

"Emma said she'd run the business. I'm going."

"You're only twelve years old. You can't travel to Capitol City alone," said my father.

"Laird's going to take me," I said confidently.

"I don't know any Laird," said my mom.

"Yeah, you are not going with some stranger," said my dad with finality.

"You guys are lame," I said as I stood up and ran upstairs to my room and slammed the door.

About twenty minutes later, my mom came upstairs and knocked on the door. "Go away," I said.

"Biff is here. He wants to talk to you."

I reluctantly opened the door and walked past my mom without looking at her and clomped down the stairs. When I got to the ground floor Biff was standing there looking somewhat nervous.

"What is it?" I asked impatiently.

Biff began haltingly. "Hurr, well, I was thinking, that, well…. Anyway, I'm upset about what Clayton did too, and my parents said they'd take me to Capitol City tomorrow when they take Claire back. Do you want to come?"

This was actually perfect. My parents would have to let me go with Biff and his family. They were responsible adults.

"Yeah that sounds great I'd love to come. Let me ask my parents."

I walked into the kitchen where my parents were both still sitting at the table. "Did you hear that? Biff and his family are going to Capitol City tomorrow. Would you mind if I rode along with them?"

"Well, I guess they are acceptable. They've been to Capitol City and back dozens of times," said my mom reluctantly.

"Make sure you pay your fair share," said my dad. "Now that you have all those emeralds, you can at least pay for your meals and any hotels you have to stay at. It is a overnight trip after all."

I smiled. "Thanks guys. I'm sorry I was such a jerk earlier."

"Don't worry, we were twelve years old once too, dear," said my mom, offering a kind smile.

I left the kitchen and went back to Biff. "It's a deal. What time are we leaving tomorrow?"

"Probably about 10:00 in the morning. Be at my house by 9:30 so we can get your stuff packed properly in our cart."

"Okay, Biff, thanks. We need to get to the bottom of this and figure out why Clayton would steal from us."

Biff nodded. "Yeah, I knew he was as greedy as the next villager, but I didn't expect he would steal from someone so blatantly."

And with that, Biff left and I shut the door behind him.

Day 24 – Just after Midnight

After Biff left, I packed all my clothes so that all I had to do was wake up in the morning, have breakfast, and walk over to Biff's house.

I'd been asleep for about three hours when I heard a soft tapping at my window. I thought it was strange because my room is on the second floor and so for someone to tap on the window, they would have to get up on the roof.

At first I thought it was just a bird or something and ignored it. But then the tapping grew louder and I could hear a pattern in the tapping. It sounded like something a person would make.

I cautiously got out of bed and went to my window and lit a torch to see what was out there. I was startled to see Emma standing on the roof and tapping at the window.

She whispered, "Open the window. There's a zombie below me and it won't go away until it can't see me."

I opened the window and let her in. "What are you doing out so late? Aren't you afraid the zombies and skeletons and spiders are going to get you?"

She shrugged. "They're pretty stupid, really. If you just pay attention you can always hide from them or run away."

I sat down on the edge of my bed while Emma sat down on a chair in the corner of my room.

"So, why are you out so late?" I asked.

"I think I want to go to Capitol City with you and confront Clayton. This is my business too and, in fact, it's my technology that he stole. I think I should be there."

"Well, I guess I don't mind the business being closed while we are gone. Are your parents okay with you going?"

Emma looked down at the floor and without raising her head said, "Yes, hurr. Yes, they are."

I sat there for a few moments and then said, "Okay. Well are you going to go back to your house now, or should I let my parents know you are here so you can sleep on the couch downstairs?"

Emma suddenly started laughing.

At first it was her normal high-pitched laugh but then it became deeper and slower and more maniacal. I was starting to get a little freaked out. I'd never heard her laugh like that. Come to think of it, I'd never heard *anyone* laugh like that.

When the laugh went on for about 15 seconds I stood up from the bed and was going to go over to Emma to see if she was okay. But, at that moment, her head bolted upright and she stared at me with glowing red evil eyes.

Oh. My. Notch!

She stopped laughing and lunged for me and began to claw my face. I could feel her fingers digging into my skin and I screamed and screamed and screamed.

And then I woke up.

It was only a dream.

I sat up in bed covered with sweat.

The stress of the last few days must've been messing with my mind.

I can't believe I thought Emma had scratched my face.

I sat there and finally caught my breath and stopped sweating. But, then I looked down on the sheet in front of me and saw little droplets of blood!

I got up and ran to the mirror. I held up a torch so that the light would reflect on my face. There were scratches that were oozing blood!

Had Emma really been there? Or, had I just scratched myself in my dream?

I looked back at the mirror to check my scratches again. But, instead of my face, I saw something else. I saw...

As I looked into the face of what could only be the legendary and mythical Entity 303, I suddenly felt the same evil vibration I had felt when I was being dragged to my death by the squid.

Could it have been Entity 303 and not an Evoker who had turned the squid evil?

My mind was racing.

It was too much.

I started to shut down.

I screamed and passed out.

END of Book 3

DIARY OF A SURFER VILLAGER

Book 4

(an unofficial Minecraft book)

Day 24 – Morning

I woke up to the feeling of my face bouncing on something. I wasn't sure exactly what it was.

Could Entity 303 have returned? Was he hitting me with some sort of magical power that only he knows how to control?

I then began to hear a strange, formless sound. Initially, it sounded like screaming or the angry voice of some sort of demonic ghast.

After a few more seconds, I finally realized the voice was saying "Jimmy! Jimmy!"

I shook my head slightly and cracked open my eyes and saw that my mom was standing over me slapping my face. Not hard. It was not abuse or anything. She was just trying to get my attention.

"Mom, stop slapping me. Hurrr," I said groggily.

She stopped and stood upright. "You are so sleepy, I thought something might be wrong. I've been trying to wake you up for about five minutes. I've been slapping your face for the last fifteen seconds. I was about to call a doctor!"

I sat up and shook my head some more to clear the cave spider cobwebs from my mind.

I thought about telling my mom about the vision. The strange dream with Emma and Entity 303 – *was* he just a dream? – but I knew that if I told her she would not let me go with Biff and his family to Capitol City. So, instead, I told her, "I think I might've stayed up too late thinking about Capitol City. I must not have gotten enough sleep."

My mom put her hands on her hips and said, "You need to be more conscientious about how much sleep you get. Make sure you get enough sleep during your trip. Don't forget, even though you will be with Biff and his family, you could still run into zombies or skeletons. You need to have your wits about you."

Dude! What a "mom" speech!

"I know, Mom, I know."

"Well, come down for breakfast soon. You have to be over at Biff's house in about 30 minutes."

"Okay, Mom," I said as I stood up and went over to my closet to get a clean brown robe to put on for the day. My mom went back downstairs to finish making breakfast. I could smell the delightful aromas of apple pies and pork chops rising from the first floor of the house.

A few minutes later, I was dressed and had fixed my hair.

BEFORE   **AFTER**

"Hurrr. Ready to face the world," I mumbled to myself as I snapped my fingers and pointed at my reflection in the mirror.

When I got downstairs my dad and mom were both sitting at the table. I grabbed two slices of apple pie, a pork chop, sliced watermelon, and a glass of water. While I was eating, my dad said, "Are you ready for the big trip?"

My mouth was full so, rather than speaking with my mouth full and risking a choking episode, I just shrugged noncommittally.

"I remember my first trip to Capitol City," said my dad. "It is a mind blowing place. It's probably one hundred times bigger than our village, and we probably have the biggest village in all of Minecraft."

I looked up at my dad. Could he be serious about how much bigger Capitol City was? I'd seen a few pictures of Capitol City, and I knew it was really flashy and had multistory buildings and bright torchlight everywhere, but I guess I never really thought about the scale of the place.

"I remember the first time I went there," said my mom. "My parents took me when I was 14 years old. We went to see a musical called *From Here to the Nether*. It was about two people who fell in love but then get separated by a zombie pigman who takes the woman down to the Nether as a prisoner and then the man has to find her and save her. Hurrr. It was so romantic."

I stuck my tongue out and shook my head and made a barfing noise. "I'm glad you guys never drag me to something so gross."

My mom smacked my shoulder playfully with the back of her hand. "Jimmy, you need to grow up."

I shrugged again. I went back to eating my food. I stuffed my face for a few more minutes.

Here's another one of those strange expressions: "to stuff one's face." It sounds as though you're taking your face off and holding it like a sack and then pushing things inside of it. That seems like a very bizarre way to treat your face. Plus, it doesn't make any sense. If stuffing your face means eating a lot of food, shouldn't the expression be "stuff your stomach" or "stuff your gut" or something like that? I just don't get how these expressions come to be.

When I was finished eating, I told my parents that I was ready to go. They both gave me a hug, my mom gave me a kiss on the cheek, and they wished me good luck. I picked up the travel bag I had packed the night before and walked over to Biff's house a few blocks away.

When I arrived at Biff's house, Emma was sitting on a bench underneath an apple tree in the front yard. When she saw me, she stood up, brushed the dust from her brown robe, came over and said, "I wanted to make sure I said goodbye before you left."

"Thanks," I said, smiling as I set my bag on the ground.

I looked over toward the house and saw Biff on his porch waving to me. I saw Claire standing inside the house through a window. She was talking to Biff's mother. She looked over and, seeing that I had arrived, scowled at me and then turned away.

Biff walked over and said, "Is that the bag you're bringing?"

I lifted the bag up and shook it. "Yes. I've got a few days worth of clothes in here and some snacks. I hope that's enough."

"I'm sure it will be enough. Besides, we will be staying with my cousins' family, and they have tons of money and will feed us all kinds of great stuff."

Although I thought such an arrangement might be a bit awkward, given that both Claire and Clayton would be living in the same house, I said, "That's awesome!"

Biff reached out and grabbed the handle of my bag. "Here, give it to me. I'll make sure it gets packed in our cart. After you're done talking to Emma, come over to the cart and we will leave."

As Biff walked away carrying my bag, I glanced around to make sure no one was within earshot and said, "Emma, I have to tell you about this crazy dream that I had yesterday. Hurrr."

"Really? How crazy was it?"

"Well, you were in it. I thought I was awake and I heard a knocking on my window in the middle of the night. The dream seemed so real. I went to the window, and you were standing there and told me let you in."

Emma looked at me like I was stupid. "How could you think it was real? What would I be doing out at midnight with all the zombies and skeletons and spiders?"

I shrugged. "I don't know. It was a dream, but I thought it was real but it was a dream, so it was a dream, even though it didn't seem like a dream. Hurrr. Dreams are weird."

She shook her head. "Anyway, continue."

"Anyway, hurrr, so I let you in the house and you were telling me you wanted to come with me to Capitol City to confront Clayton and then suddenly you started laughing like a maniac, your eyes turned red, and you attacked me and scratched my face and made it bleed. But then I woke up."

"And there wasn't any blood, right?" asked Emma in a know-it-all voice.

"Actually, my face was bleeding. Hurrr. But, by then you had disappeared and I realized it had been a dream and I must've scratched myself so I went over to the mirror to see what my face looked like, and when I looked into the mirror I saw Entity 303 looking back at me!"

Emma took in a sharp breath in shock. "Are you sure it was Entity 303?"

"Yes, it was Entity 303 for sure, but then I passed out. So I'm not sure if I saw Entity 303 in another dream or if he really was there and I passed out from shock."

Emma put her finger to her lips and thought about what I just told her. "Do you believe Entity 303 really exists, or is he just a fairy tale created to scare little kids?" she asked.

"Well, I've heard a lot of stories about him. I mean, I know Herobrine is real because so many people have seen him and there are actually history books and diaries written about his misdeeds." I paused and thought for a moment. "But, Entity 303 seems much more mysterious. Part of me wants to believe it was just a myth and I saw him because it was my only way of processing the fear I was feeling in my dream. But part of me thinks he really does exist and he actually appeared in my room."

Emma didn't seem to believe my logic. "Even if Entity 303 is real, why would he appear to you? I've always heard that Entity 303 is about causing problems for players not NPCs. Hurrr. Why would he bother messing with a villager?"

Obviously, I had no idea why Entity 303 would appear to me. "I don't know, maybe the same person who possessed that squid wanted the scare me and sent Entity 303 in a vision."

"Scare you from what?"

Again, I had no idea. "I wish I knew."

Emma laughed. She reached over and pulled me to her and gave me a hug. "You're so crazy, Jimmy." She stopped her hug and pushed me away gently.

"Maybe I am."

"Anyway, don't worry about the Surf 'n Snack while you're gone. If I need any help running it, I'll hire a few kids to do some work. We should make quite a few emeralds in the next few weeks before school starts."

I nodded. The thought of all those emeralds coming in made me happy again. My greedy villager self was asserting its power. And for once I didn't try to push it away.

"Just be careful about Claire," said Emma in a quiet conspiratorial voice. "I'm not sure she has anything to do with Clayton stealing our idea, but she's always talking about how little she knows about everything, which makes me think maybe she actually knows a lot about a lot of things. Hurrr. It's a convenient cover story."

I looked over at Claire who was still talking to Biff's mother inside the house. *Could she really be that conniving and duplicitous?* On the surface, she seemed so nice. She even gave me the multicolored robe, which was now packed in my bag and which I planned to wear the first day we were in Capitol City.

I looked back at Emma. "I'll be careful. I haven't detected any vibes that makes me think she's an evil person, but you're right, you never know."

Emma smiled and waved at me and said goodbye and walked away. I put my hands across my chest and tucked each of them into the opposite sleeve, like we villagers do when we are bored.

I walked over toward the cart and told Biff I was ready to go. Biff went inside and got his parents and Claire. As she passed, Claire nodded at me but did not say, "Hi." I nodded to her wordlessly. I guess she was still mad at me for yelling at her the other day.

I sat in the back of the cart with Biff and the baggage, while Biff's parents and Claire sat in the front area which had padded seats.

I got comfortable on top of my bag and told Biff that I felt kind of tired and was hoping I could take a quick nap. He said he understood and told me he'd wake me up for lunch.

"Thanks, man, I appreciate it." I said.

The last thing I heard was Biff's dad telling the horses to get moving and the snap of the reins. Then I fell asleep.

Day 24 – Afternoon

The next thing I knew Biff was gently kicking my foot with his own. I stirred awake and asked groggily, "What's up?"

"We're stopping for lunch. Come on, let's look around. My mom said she'd get the lunch ready."

I nodded to Biff and stretched. I felt a lot better since I took the nap. I usually thought of naps as things for super-old villager grandparents, but I have to say that I now understand why people like naps so much.

I hopped out of the back of the covered cart and saw that we had parked on the top of a small hill underneath a tree. Claire was sitting against the tree looking through a paperback Minecraft diary she had brought with her. It looked like one about a Minecraft bat named Jasper.

Biff's mother was busy putting together some food for lunch and Biff's father was caring for the horses.

Biff pointed away from the tree and said, "Look at that. Isn't it awesome!"

I looked to where Biff was pointing. "So, we've been traveling through a savannah biome?"

"Yes, about an hour outside of the village it transitions from a forest biome to a plains biome and then to a savannah biome. The cool thing is that you can see lots of wildlife."

I scanned the distance and saw that Biff was correct. There was a herd of majestic llamas slowly migrating somewhere. I also noticed a similarly majestic wolf stalking the herd at a discrete distance, hoping for a tasty snack.

Biff tapped me on the arm and said, "Let's go look around a bit. It looks like it is going to be a few more minutes before my mom finishes making lunch."

I followed Biff down the hill a bit and we saw lots of flowers blooming and all sorts of different plants growing. We saw a few piglets wandering in the grass, but they ran away as we approached. They probably thought we meant them harm, but we did not.

We had walked a little further when I spotted a bunny. I had never seen a bunny in the wild, only in cages at pet stores. It was pretty cool. I started to sneak up on the bunny to get as close as I could. I thought maybe I could pet it or at least touch it and maybe feed it a carrot or something.

The bunny rabbit sat still as I approached. His back was turned to me so I don't think he could see me, but I was surprised that he did not hear me because I was only a few feet away.

I kept creeping closer and closer until the bunny was within arm's reach. I slowly stretched out my left hand and touched it on its back at which point it turned around and hissed at me, at which point I saw it had glowing red evil eyes!

Behind me, Biff screamed. "Oh my Notch! It's eyes are just like the eyes of the squid that tried to drown you!"

I continued to stare at the red eyes of the rabbit transfixed. And then, just as quickly as the rabbit had turned toward me, it's eyes faded to a normal color and it hopped away rapidly.

I looked over at Biff and asked, "What do you think that was?"

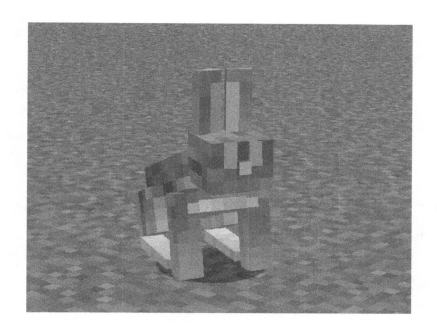

Biff was shaken. His voice was cracking with fear as he responded, "I ... I ... hurr ... don't ... know."

"I don't know either. That was really weird. If you hadn't seen the glowing red eyes also, I would've thought I was imagining it," I said.

I didn't want to tell Biff what I was thinking. I didn't want to tell him about the research Emma and I had done about vexes and Evokers and possession. I did not want Biff to be scared, but even more importantly, I did not want him to tell Clayton or Claire or any of his other relatives that I suspected Clayton might be in league with an Evoker.

I decided to change the subject. "Say, Biff, do you think lunch is ready?"

Biff nodded. "Yeah, we should probably head back."

On the way back to camp, I noticed some wild watermelons growing and I picked a couple of them and took them with us.

Claire was still sitting under the tree but now had some cookies and a roasted chicken leg she was eating. I walked up to her and said, "Hey, we found some watermelons. Do you want a piece?"

Claire didn't say anything but simply scowled. I took that as "no."

I shook my head as I walked to where everyone else was sitting. I put the watermelons on the table. "I found some watermelons, if anybody wants some."

Biff grabbed a watermelon and cracked it open and took a few bites. Then he said, "That was nice of you to offer Claire some watermelon. She won't stay mad at you forever. Claire is a good egg."

And yet again, another one of those expressions I will never understand. Why would you compare anyone to an egg in the first place, much less to a good or bad egg? By "good egg," did people mean that you weren't a rotten egg and so you didn't stink? Or did it mean you were a perfect oval shape? Or did it mean you could break easily? The ridiculousness of language continues to astound me.

Claire

Good egg

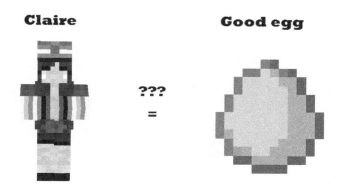

???

=

We remained under the tree for another thirty minutes while we finished our lunch and then packed it away.

Before we started moving again, Biff's father told us all that it would probably be about another three or four hours until we got to the village of Creeper Junction where we would be spending the night. He told us to be on the lookout for any creepers from now on, as they tended to be more common place in this part of the Overworld. If we saw a creeper we were to let him know so he could redirect the cart and avoid it.

Biff and I got comfortable in the back of the cart, keeping vigil for creepers, while Claire traveled in comfort in the front of the cart with Biff's parents.

Day 24 – Evening

We arrived at the village of Creeper Junction just as the square sun was beginning to set over the western horizon. We'd seen about five creepers on the way, but because we had been vigilant they were easily avoided.

During the journey, Biff's father told us the story of how Creeper Junction was founded. Apparently, several hundred years ago a group of villagers had been banished from Capitol City because they had been found to have been worshiping a God who looked like a creeper rather than Notch. As they wandered in their exile, they faced all sorts of hardships such as nighttime zombie attacks, daytime husk raids, and even creeper attacks (*the irony!*). As they were giving up hope of ever finding a place to settle, they came across two creepers who for some reason walked directly into each other and exploded.

The explosion blew a hole in the earth which revealed a large underground lake. The village is built around this lake and still draws water from it. Many of the exiles in Creeper Junction still worship what they believed to be the creeper god. However, as it has been several hundred years since their exile, many of the villagers in Creeper Junction today have given up the religion of their ancestors or moved to Creeper Junction from elsewhere and do not share the same religious beliefs.

Now, the village was a trading post because it was equidistant from several other villages and Capitol City, making a perfect stopping off point, which is what we were now doing. Because Creeper Junction was a transit point for so many villagers and players, there were dozens of inns where we could stay.

"Our favorite hotel is the Shaking Creeper Inn," said Biff's mother as we traveled. "They have very reasonable prices and some of the best apple pie I've ever had."

Biff's father let out a sigh of delight. "Oh, yes, they have good apple pie all right. And there's always a lot of people there so you can have a good conversation if that's what you want to do."

I didn't really care where we stayed as long as it was safe from creepers and zombies.

When we arrived at the Shaking Creeper Inn, a valet approached and took the reins of the cart from Biff's father. We quickly unpacked the bags in the back of the cart and the valet took the cart to the stables where the horses would be boarded for the night. We walked inside the lobby where Biff's father secured two rooms for the night: one where Biff, his father and I would sleep and one where Biff's mother and Claire would sleep.

We went up to the rooms and dropped off our bags. After washing my face and using the bathroom, we all went back downstairs for dinner.

I couldn't believe it, but Claire had actually changed her clothes before dinner! She had on a new multicolored shirt and a pair of black baggy pants, which appeared to be a style adopted from the common outfits of players.

I didn't know any villagers who accentuated their pants because the robes normally came down almost to their feet. It was strange to see the peculiar styles that must be common in Capitol City.

In fact, many people in the dining room were staring at Claire because they had never seen anyone wear clothing like this. The one exception was another girl about Claire's age who was wearing a multicolored robe and had some sort of sparkly ribbon tied her hair. She walked over to Claire and said, "Oh my Notch, I love your pants and your shirt. You must be from Capitol City like me. My name is Cynthia."

Claire smiled. "Finally, someone who understands. Yes, I am. My name is Claire Dretsky."

The girl gasped. "Are you from *THE* Dretsky family? The business tycoons?"

Claire nodded. You could tell she was enjoying all the attention.

"Wow, it must be really great to be super rich. I'm glad I got to meet you," said Cynthia before she turned and walked away to go have dinner with her family at a another table.

Claire turned around and then sat at the table with us. I looked at her.

Was she as shallow as she seemed? Did she just care about wearing fancy clothes and getting praise from random strangers?

She didn't seem like that when I first met her in Zombie Bane. But, once I called her brother out as a thief, she changed. Now that we were getting closer to Capitol City, she seemed to be changing even more. I wasn't sure what to make of it.

Just as Biff's mother had said, the food in the Inn was quite good. Not as good as my mom's food, but close.

After dinner, Biff's parents told us we all needed to go to sleep right away. We'd be getting up at first light in order to arrive at Capitol City before dark the next day. After we returned to our room, I spent a few minutes getting my clothes ready for tomorrow and then got ready for bed.

I walked in the bathroom and shut the door. I took my robe off so that I wouldn't get any water on the front of it when I washed my face and brushed my teeth. As I brushed my teeth, I looked in the mirror to make sure that the foam was sufficiently lathered.

Once I had finished, I spit the toothpaste in the sink and then washed my face with water.

I grabbed a towel to dry my face. Once my face was sufficiently dry, I looked in the mirror to make sure there weren't any dirt streaks on it. But, looking back at me from the mirror was not my own face, but the face of Herobrine!

I closed my eyes and shook my head thinking I was just imagining things, with all the weird stuff I'd seen lately, it wouldn't have surprised me if my brain would now start making this stuff up just to mess with me. Herobrine was still there when I opened my eyes again.

"What ... hurr ... what do you want?" I asked with a trembling voice.

Herobrine smirked. "You, Jimmy Slade, will have to find the answer to that question yourself."

I was about to ask him something else when his image vanished and I was left staring at my own terrified face.

Shaken, I replaced the towel and put my robe back on. I walked out of the bathroom and went to bed without saying a word to anyone about what I had seen. Or ... *thought* I had seen.

Day 25 – Morning

Despite the fright I had from Herobrine's mysterious appearance last night, I slept soundly without any dreams or nightmares.

Some might say that I slept like a log. I've pondered this bizarre expression many times. While it is true that logs rest on the ground without any movement or activity no matter what disturbs them, one cannot really say they are sleeping. They are inanimate objects that do not wake or sleep. So, to "sleep like a log" to me means that you would have to be dead for it to actually apply. And, since when villagers pass away in Minecraft, they turn into puffs of smoke, the expression made absolutely no sense.

Anyway ... when I woke up, Biff and his father were already dressed. Brown robes, of course.

Biff said, "Hurry up, Jimmy, get your robe on and let's go have a quick breakfast before we leave."

I nodded my understanding and quickly pulled on a brown robe and pushed my hair to the side with one hand so it didn't look too crazy.

When we got down to the dining area at the Inn, Claire and Biff's mother were already eating some fried eggs and pork chops. I ordered a fried egg, pork chop, a slice of apple pie, and a glass of water.

Everyone at the table was still pretty tired so we didn't talk about much other than how our food tasted. Everyone said the food tasted pretty good.

When the waiter brought the bill, I gave Biff's dad three emeralds to pay for my share.

"You don't have to pay for this, Jimmy," he said.

"Oh no, I insist. My dad told me I should pay my share of the food, and I agree. You're giving me a free ride to the Capitol City, so it's the least I could do."

Biff's dad smiled and grabbed the emeralds and put them in his pocket. "I appreciate it, Jimmy. That's very thoughtful."

I looked across the table at Claire who rolled her eyes. She obviously wasn't going to offer to pay her own way. She was used to having other people pay for everything.

The one thing I thought was strange was that Claire was wearing a brown robe today. She looked like any other villager. But then I saw it. On the upper left side of the robe just below the collar, was a small creeper emblem with each square of the creeper's body colored with the colors of a rainbow.

"What is that?" I said, pointing at the rainbow creeper.

Claire looked where I was pointing and realized I meant the logo on her robe. "Oh, it's a new designer in Capitol City. It's called the Rainbow Creeper line and only the most fashionable people have it."

"But it looks just like a regular brown robe except for there's a little tiny rainbow creeper on it. How is that fashionable?" I asked, completely confused.

Claire sighed and shook her head. "If you have to ask, you'll never understand."

I had no response to that.

Biff's parents informed us they were ready to leave and told us to go grab our bags and bring them downstairs to put into the cart. We did so and met them out front where Biff's father gave a five-emerald tip to the valet who had brought the cart around. We loaded our bags in the back. Biff and I climbed in and, to my surprise, Claire followed.

"Don't you want to sit up front?" I asked.

"It was boring riding with the adults. Do you mind if I sit back there? I know we haven't been getting along, but I thought it might be fun to look out the back of the cart for a change," said Claire.

I shrugged. "I don't care. There's plenty of room."

Biff smiled. "Sure, Claire, you can tell us all about Capitol City before we get there."

Claire climbed in and took a seat, leaning against her bag. "Capital City is really just like any other village except it's a lot bigger and has much brighter torchlight. There is more money in Capitol City too, but most residents are like any other villagers. They're greedy and just want to make as much money as possible and stockpile emeralds."

I was confused. "Then how come people from Capitol City always talk about how much cooler they are than everybody else? How come they always wear fashionable clothes and act like plain brown robes are stupid?"

Claire sighed and looked a little embarrassed. "You know, there's so much money in Capitol City that people don't know what to do with it. Instead of just saving it or helping out poor villagers, they would rather spend it on stupid things. I mean, I know that I spend a lot of money on clothes and so I'm guilty of it too, that's just how it is. Villagers are basically just selfish."

I could not believe I was hearing this from Claire's mouth. She seemed so shallow last night when she was talking to the girl from Capitol City about clothes. Now, she suddenly sounds like some kind of philosopher who wants people to share money with each other? It did not make any sense.

The cart began to move as we began the remainder of our journey to Capitol City. Biff's father reminded us to keep a lookout for creepers for the next couple of hours while we were still near Creeper Junction. He said that as we approached Capitol City the odds of seeing a creeper would become much lower because so many players came to Capitol City and killed creepers on the way there and back that creepers generally avoided a fairly wide radius around Capitol City.

We told Biff's father we understood and would keep a lookout. Then we resumed chatting.

"Claire, I don't understand you," I said. "I mean, it seems like you are really nice sometimes and then other times you seem really mean and, well, pretty shallow and self-centered. I just don't get it."

Claire laughed. "You haven't met very many girls have you?" she said with a smile. "Actually, it's not just us girls who have different emotions and outlooks, all people do. Look, Jimmy, I like you. You seem like a cool guy. But when you insulted my brother Clayton, I got really upset at you and I'm just finally starting to not be angry anymore."

"I'm sorry about that, but I was really upset because it's pretty obvious Clayton stole the wave technology that Emma invented so he could make his own money from it," I said.

Claire nodded. She picked a piece of dirt off the front of her brown robe and flicked it out the back of the cart. "You know, I want to tell you something. I'll deny it if you ever mention it, but it's true." She paused and then continued. "Clayton is the greediest person in my family."

Biff gasped. "Even greedier than your father!"

Claire pursed her lips and said, "Much more."

I was confused again. "What do you mean, Biff? How greedy is their father?"

Biff looked at me like I was an idiot. "You know they're from the Dretsky family right? The Dretskys are billionaires. They've been the greediest villager family for the last 200 years. They've amassed such a gigantic fortune that their family alone controls one half of all villager wealth in the entire Overworld! And, most of that was amassed during the lifetime of Claire's father and grandfather."

I had to say I was impressed. I knew Claire came from a rich family but I didn't know her dad was a billionaire.

"So, should you even be riding in this cart with us?" I asked. "Shouldn't you have some sort of entourage and a bunch of bodyguards?"

Claire laughed. "That's stupid. What is there to be afraid of? No one is stupid enough to kidnap me. If they did, they know that my father would find them and take care of them, if you know what I mean."

I shivered at the implication.

She continued, "I'm probably safer than you."

I thought about her logic for a minute. Maybe she was safer. I had no idea since I wasn't a billionaire. I was, at most, a thousand-aire after splitting the earnings of the Surf 'n Snack with Emma.

"Okay," I said, "so, lots of people in Claire's family are next-level greedy. What makes Clayton so special?"

Claire sat up and cracked her neck from side to side and then arched her back to get the kinks out of it from sitting in the back of the cart with us peasants.

"Gee," she said as she rubbed her neck, "maybe an entourage would be nice. This cart is really uncomfortable. Anyway, back to Clayton. When we were young children, he told me one time that he wanted to have more money than father. That is a lot of money. I didn't believe him. I just thought he was talking big like a lot of kids do, but he meant it.

"From the time he was five years old, all he cared about was making money. He would steal it, borrow it, or earn it. Father even called him a prodigy. Let's just say that there is no line Clayton won't cross in the pursuit of money." When Claire finished, she looked down at the floorboards of the cart and picked at a splinter of wood.

I looked at Claire. I could tell she was ... what was it? Ashamed? It would be difficult to have a brother who was so greedy and unprincipled about his greed, especially when your father encouraged it.

Although Emma did not believe in vibes, I was getting good vibes from Claire at that moment. It really seemed like she thought that her brother was out of line, and she wished that he wasn't quite so greedy. I guess she really was a good egg. It was then that I thought I would ask her.

"Claire, have you ever seen anything weird when you look in the mirror?" I asked.

Claire looked up at me quickly with a flash of anger in her eyes. "What are you saying? That I'm hideous and ugly?"

I put my hands out in front of me and shook them to indicate that she had totally misunderstood me. Actually, Claire was quite the opposite of ugly. "No, last night at the Inn. I'm just...," I stammered. "It's just that I've seen some strange things over the past few days."

"The rabbit?" asked Biff.

"That, but so much more," I said.

Biff looked at me in shock. "What you talking about? You never said anything to me."

"I didn't want to bother anyone. I thought maybe I was imagining it. I still might be, but I just wanted to ask Claire and you too I guess, whether you've seen anything strange in mirrors lately."

"I haven't," said Biff quickly.

Claire looked at me with a curious expression on her face. I could tell she had something to say, but she wasn't sure if she should reveal it.

"Why?" she asked curiously. "What have you been seeing in mirrors lately?"

And now for the big reveal....

"I saw Entity 303 before we left Zombie Bane and I saw Herobrine last night."

I actually felt a wave of relief letting them know my secret.

Both Claire and Biff gasped at this revelation.

"Why didn't you tell me?" asked Biff. "If Herobrine is around, we all could be in danger."

I shook my head. "I don't think so. He appeared only for a brief moment. He didn't make any threats. He said something strange like there is a puzzle I needed to figure out, but I have no idea what puzzle it could be."

Claire sighed. "I don't know anything about a puzzle, but I can tell you that the night before we left Zombie Bane, I saw something strange in the mirror too. I thought I was only imagining things but maybe I wasn't. I was brushing my hair before going to sleep and when I looked in the mirror, I saw a witch looking back at me. I blinked my eyes hard and the witch disappeared. Until you asked me that question just now, I had assumed I was just really tired and hallucinating."

"Ah, man! Ah, geez! Hurrr. What could this mean, Jimmy?" asked Biff in a panic.

"I have no idea, but I think it might relate to the squid and bunny rabbit."

What bunny rabbit?" asked Claire.

I told her about the possessed bunny Biff and I had seen the other day at lunch time.

"That's pretty weird," said Claire. "Why do you think it's related?"

Honestly, it was only a hunch. I had no evidence that anything was related to anything else, but I couldn't shake the feeling that Clayton had something to do with this. I couldn't shake the feeling that there was a sinister Evoker on the loose. I couldn't shake the feeling that I got really bad vibes from Clayton but not from Claire. I decided to tell her. Well, not tell her, but explore the possibility.

"Claire, does your family know any Evokers?"

Claire was instantaneously offended by my question. She smacked her hand on the floorboards of the cart loudly and said, "Of course not! How could you ask such a thing?!? That's like saying we'd invite Herobrine or Entity 303 to a dinner party."

I froze. Why had she chosen to use those two creatures as an example? Was it just because I had mentioned them recently or was or something else going on? Had Entity 303 and Herobrine been attending dinner parties at the Dretsky house?

Well, if they had, I don't think Claire knew about it. I was still getting good vibes from her, though now they were angry vibes.

I tried to explain. "Well, I've done some research and I figured out that Evokers can use vexes to possess animals and other mobs. I have a theory that an Evoker possessed the squid to ruin my surf park business and I guess the Evoker could've possessed the bunny rabbit briefly to spy on me."

Claire shook her head and looked at me like I was a complete fool. "Where do you come up with this stuff, Jimmy? How can this even be something you're thinking about? And what does it have to do with me or my family?"

I sighed. "I've seen evidence that this has been done in the past. I've seen books about it."

"Yeah, so? Why do you think my family has anything to do with it?"

"Don't you think it's strange that just as the squid closes down my surf park, Clayton leaves and then opens his own surf park in Capitol City?"

I saw the blood drain from Claire's face. "But ... hurr ... but ... that's ridiculous."

I could tell she did not believe her own words. I could see her mentally struggling for another explanation, but not finding one. She knew her brother Clayton was the ultimate amoral greedy villager who only cared about money and would do *anything* to get it. She'd said it herself. She couldn't decide if Clayton would be willing to cross the line into the use of occult magic and possession of other living beings.

"I … just … don't say anything to Clayton or my father about this," said Claire. "I don't know how they'd react."

I nodded. "I wasn't going to. But, I was going to try to gather some evidence about it."

"This is crazy," said Biff. "I can't believe my cousin might be involved with Evokers! I hope you're wrong, but…." He didn't have to finish his sentence. We all knew Clayton was capable of it.

Day 25 – Afternoon

After the discussion about Clayton, we all were quiet for a couple of hours. We all were thinking about what it would mean if Clayton were involved in the strange occult world of the Evokers. I think we all reached the same conclusion that it would not end well ... for someone.

We stopped for a brief lunch. I didn't want to do any exploring. I was afraid of finding other possessed creature, maybe a piglet or a chicken.

When we finished eating, we moved on. This time, Claire sat up front with the adults. Biff and I sat in the back and continued our silent ride to Capitol City.

Towards late afternoon, Biff's father yelled, "I can see it. Capitol City straight ahead."

I stood up in the back of the cart and opened the hatch at the top to look at Capitol City. I couldn't believe what I was seeing. It was awesome.

The city itself seemed to spread from horizon to horizon. The buildings were ten, fifteen, even twenty stories tall, and I could see mine cart tracks running between the top floors of the buildings like a roller coaster. But, it was not an amusement park ride, it was just necessary transportation in a city filled with hundreds of thousands of villagers.

I saw in front of us the road became wider and wider, and I could see hundreds of other carts and villagers and players walking to and from Capitol City.

This was what was meant by the word metropolis.

My mind was completely blown.

Day 25 – Evening

We got inside Capitol City's walls as the sun was beginning to set. It took us another fifteen minutes to drive through the enormous streets before we reached Claire's house, at the top of a large hill.

Well, maybe "house" is not the right word. It was more of a mansion. Or maybe it was more like five or six mansions put together. I thought it was an office building as we were approaching it.

We pulled into the circular driveway and stopped. Two valets came out, one to hold the horses and another one to help everyone out of the cart. A third servant came out to gather the baggage onto a small rolling cart.

The servant carrying my bag asked me if there was anything else that I needed. I said, "I'd like to talk to Clayton as soon as possible."

Claire shot a look at me, warning me against what I was thinking of doing. But I didn't care.

"I'm sorry sir, but Clayton is currently on a business trip to the Nether gathering raw materials.

He should return tomorrow. I will leave him a note to let him know you wanted to see him."

"Thanks, brah," I said.

The servant looked shocked that I would treat him with such familiarity. In response to my attempt to treat him like a bro, he said, "If you all would follow me I will lead you to your rooms."

Claire waved goodbye to us and said, "Dinner is in about an hour. I'll see you all then."

We all waved to Claire and then followed the servant to our rooms.

I was expecting to have to share a room with Biff, but Biff and I each had our own room, connected by an adjoining bathroom. Biff's parents had a separate room next door.

After the servant put my bag on the bed he asked, "Would you like me to unpack your clothes for you, sir?"

I was not used to being treated like this. I told him that I would do it myself and reached in my pocket and pulled out a few emeralds for a tip.

He looked at the emeralds as if he were offended by the very offer. "Sir, that is not necessary. Mr. Dretsky takes care of all my needs." And with a flourish and a bow the servant left the room.

I unpacked my clothes, which amounted to three brown robes, one multicolored robe, and four pairs of pants. When I was done, I walked through the bathroom into Biff's bedroom, which was an exact duplicate of mine. Biff was sitting on the bed admiring how it felt. "This is the most amazing bed I've ever felt. It's ... hurrr ... firm yet very soft. It's like floating on a cloud."

I slapped my head. "How would you know what it's like to float on a cloud?"

"It's just an expression, dude."

"Whatever," I said. "Hurrr, this place is amazing! I can't believe how huge this house is. If you put our two-bedrooms together it's like half as big as my house in Zombie Bane."

Biff nodded. "I knew Claire and Clayton's family were billionaires, but my parents never really explained to me what it meant. Now, I see."

"Yeah, parents tend to keep those sort of facts from kids. I don't know if parents are embarrassed because they aren't billionaires or if they just don't want their kids to get weird around people with money."

Biff shrugged. "I don't know, hurrr, villagers are so weird. On the one hand, they're greedy and want to make bunch of money, but on the other hand they hide interesting economic information from their children. It's a conundrum."

"I think you mean a 'paradox.'"

Biff looked at me out of the corner of his eyes. "You know what I mean. We don't have to have perfect diction, do we?"

I laughed. "Dude, hurrr, I'm kidding. It's still summer. We can talk dumb-ly and not get in trouble-ly with teachers." I changed the subject. "What do you think we will eat for dinner?"

Biff rubbed his chin in thought for a moment and then clicked his tongue against his teeth. "I think will probably have ... everything."

* * *

Biff was right. I had never seen so much food on one table in my life.

Interestingly, the only people at dinner were Biff's parents, Biff, Claire, and me. I knew Clayton was in the Nether, but I was surprised that Biff's parents were absent as well.

Five servants stood at a respectful distance from the table and any time a plate was empty took it away and brought a new plate and then asked what they might serve. After about an hour, I wanted to stop eating, but I felt like it would be rude to tell them to stop serving me.

Claire noticed that I was beginning to turn green because I was so bloated with food and told the servants, "I think Jimmy's had enough. Why don't you clear the table and bring dessert?"

"As you wish, Miss Claire."

Miss Claire?!? So goofy.

The servants cleared all the food and plates away while Biff's parents oooh'd and ahhh'd at how amazing the food was and how incredible it must be to have servants do everything for you.

Claire took it all in stride. She didn't seem overly arrogant about her good fortune, but she also acknowledged that she was quite fortunate. It was a delicate balancing act. I was beginning to admire her.

I leaned back in my chair and folded my hands across my bloated stomach. "I think I ate more food tonight than I've eaten in the past week. Why did you let me do that?"

Biff laughed at me. "Come on, little man, that wasn't so much food, was it?" I couldn't respond with words. All I could do was moan.

A few minutes later, the servants returned with dessert plates and silverware and a tray of desserts. These were desserts I'd never seen before. I was expecting apple pie or watermelon slices or something similar. Maybe an apple. But these were exotic and, quite frankly, strange: beetroot pie; golden apple fritters; watermelon gelato; and frozen raw rabbit on a stick encrusted with toasted pumpkin seeds. (I didn't eat the rabbit dessert; it sounded disgusting.)

When we had finished dessert, Claire stood up and said, "Well, hurrr, it's getting late. I'm going to go to bed. If you'd like anything else, let the servants know and they will get it for you. Otherwise, I'll see you in the morning. My parents and Clayton should be back."

"Are your parents with Clayton in the Nether also?" asked Biff's mother.

"No, Auntie, they aren't. The servants told me they were both at an important business meeting."

"A business meeting this late at night?" I asked.

Claire shrugged. "They go to business meetings all hours of the day and night. This is nothing unusual." And with that, Claire left the room.

I couldn't help but think it was strange that there would be business meetings during the evening and night. I knew business people had parties and such in the evenings, but they usually tried to get their business done during daylight hours, unless they were running a restaurant or a hotel or something.

Anyway, I didn't have the energy to ponder the vagaries of late-night business meetings, so I stood up and told everyone I was going to my room. I waddled away from the table, my hands on my bloated stomach.

Somehow, I made it to my room without falling over. I quickly brushed my teeth, saw nothing but myself in the mirror, and then fell asleep.

Day 26 – Morning

I woke up with first light. I felt well rested. Because I been so stuffed after dinner last night, I wasn't hungry at all. Rather than stay in bed, I decided I'd look around the house to see what interesting things there were to see.

I quickly got dressed, putting on my multicolored robe so that I'd blend in with all the cool Capitol City kids, and left my room. I walked down the hallway and came to a T-shaped intersection. I looked left and right. To the right, there were a bunch of paintings on the wall. To the left, I saw several doors leading to rooms. All of the doors were open. I'd look at the paintings later; I wanted to see what was in these rooms.

I probably wouldn't have admitted it at the time, but I was snooping. I wanted to see if I could find something to link Clayton or anyone else in his family to the possessions and evoking I'd been noticing recently. Or, perhaps, something to link them to Herobrine and Entity 303.

The first door opened into a room containing several statues. They were statues of various mobs, including zombies, skeletons, ghasts, and blazes. The statues were very well done and quite lifelike. It was almost as if the creatures had been turned to stone rather than a stone being carved away to turn into them. But, I wasn't interested in looking at statues, so I walked on.

The next door, on the right side of the corridor, opened into a room containing various games. There was a pool table, a foosball table, a pinball machine, a dartboard, and a checkers and chess set. It was too early in the morning to play games, but I thought I'd be back to play some pool later. I hadn't played pool in a few months, so it would be fun.

The next room I entered was what I had hoped to find: the library. I walked into a room that was easily the size of my parents' house. Every wall was lined floor-to-ceiling with books. There were also bookshelves throughout the center of the room. There were probably more books in here than in any one place I'd ever seen.

I walked up to the first bookshelf and to my surprise and delight, there was actually a map of the books in the room! I scanned the map and found a bookshelf labeled "Occult Books."

Oh my Notch, I can't believe this! They might actually have all the books I need to figure out the answers to my questions!

I walked quickly over to the occult book section. I noticed that they had the same book that I had looked at in Mr. Blaze's bookstore. There were also other books about Evokers, vexes, magic, potion making, Herobrine, Entity 303, myths of Minecraft, and others.

This is what the bookshelf looked like – packed:

I was so excited at my find, that I was actually physically shaking. I pulled out an old leather bound volume labeled *Human Applications of Possession* and put it down on a table and began to flip through it. I found a section about how a villager could potentially use evoking powers. It was an old text, at least 400 years old, and it didn't look like the book had been opened in a long time. I began to read.

I had just finished the first two sentences – which said "Tis a dangerous proposition to embark upon the experimental process of Evocation. To labor with vexes and the mind goo of other creatures, including villagers, is fraught with peril." – when I heard a gruff voice behind me say, "What are you doing in here?"

I turned around and saw Clayton with his hands on his hips in a power stance. He continued, "This is *my* family's library. No one gave you permission to be in here."

I quickly closed the book and shoved it back in the bookshelf. I stammered, "I'm sorry. I just ... hurrr ... got up early ... and ... thought it would be okay to walk around. I just happened upon the library and was interested."

Clayton curled his lips with disapproval and squinted his eyes at me. "And, so you find the library and then go right to the occult section?"

"Well, after the squid incident, I'm sort of interested in what happens when passive mobs get possessed."

I could tell Clayton was not expecting that response. He flinched slightly, as if taken by surprise. "What makes you think the squid was possessed? It probably just grabbed that kid because it was frightened by the surfboard."

"Biff said he saw its eyes when he saved me. They were glowing red. What else could make its eyes red other than some form of magic?"

Clayton laughed. "I'm sure there are a million things that can turn a squid's eyes red if you just knew anything about marine biology."

I suppose he could've been right, but I knew he wasn't. "Well, do you have any marine biology books I could look through?" I asked, calling his bluff.

"Yeah, there are some over here. Follow me."

I followed Clayton down one corridor then turned right then turned left down another corridor until we came to a bookshelf against the wall of the room. Clayton pointed to the bookshelf and moved his finger up and down. "All of these shelves have marine biology books on them. Look, here are four books about squids. Why don't you take them back to your room and read them?"

Now, he had called my bluff. "Okay, I'll do that. Thanks." *Lame.*

Clayton grabbed all four books and he put them in my outstretched hands. When his hand touched mine, I felt as though something had passed from him and me. It felt like something evil. Suddenly, I had the worst sense of bad vibes I'd ever felt from any one person. I didn't know if it was the close proximity to Clayton or if it was the actual touching, but I knew right then and there that Clayton was truly evil.

"Thanks, Clayton. Hurrr, I guess I'll get going," I said as I backed away from him and quickly turned toward the door of the library.

"Hey, Jimmy, isn't there something else you'd really like to talk to me about?"

I looked at him. I did want to confront him about stealing the wave machine, but it felt like he had the upper hand right now. I needed to find a better time.

"No, not really," I said unconvincingly.

"You're such a liar," said Clayton with an accusatory tone. "You want to confront me about stealing your wave technology, don't you?"

I could feel the anger rising in me. I took the books and set them on a nearby shelf. I clenched my fist and said, "Yeah, I do. I was trying to be polite and find a better time to do it, but you did steal it, didn't you? You're not even trying to hide it."

Clayton laughed. "You're so stupid, Jimmy. Emma told me everything about how the wave machine worked. I didn't have to steal anything; I was given the technology. You didn't ask me to sign a nondisclosure agreement or noncompetition agreement, so I can do whatever I want. *That's the law.* In fact, I've made a different and *better* wave park than you. We have bigger waves, stronger waves, and more varied waves. Your surf parks sucks."

I couldn't believe he was being so open about what he had done. Obviously, he had no shame about stealing the idea. So I tried something else.

"Clayton, it's not just the technology. You're going to steal all of our customers. You're already so rich, why do you have to take away business from rural villagers like me and Emma?"

Clayton laughed again. "Seriously? Dude, other than Capitol City, your surf park is the only place anyone can go to surf. I'm not going to give the technology to anyone else. And besides, no one from Capitol City would travel to Zombie Bane just to use a surf park and no one who wants to go to Zombie Bane would travel to Capitol City just to use a surf park. Look at it this way, we're not stealing each other's customers, we're creating more desire for them to go surfing."

Wait, what?

I hadn't thought about it that way. Clayton did have a good business mind, although he was exceptionally evil and greedy. I had to admit that he was probably right that in the end the existence of another wave park might actually create more desire to ride the waves at my park. I couldn't believe this, but I was agreeing with Clayton.

I scratched my head and said, "Hurrr, maybe you are right."

"Of course I'm right. I am a great businessman. You know what, I'll even put a sign up at my park that says you invented waves and that the original surf park in the Overworld is located in Zombie Bane. What do you think about that?"

I couldn't believe it! He was actually going to advertise my park at his park. This was incredible. Maybe Clayton wasn't such an evil jerk after all? Maybe my vibe sensor wasn't working? Maybe Emma was right that vibes didn't really mean much?

"Um, yeah, if you want to do that, that would be awesome."

Clayton smiled. He stuck out his hand and we shook. "It's a deal. I'll make sure that sign gets up in the next day or two."

I smiled back. "Sounds good. Say, do you think I could try your surf park today? I heard from someone that there are three different types of waves."

"No problem, but we should probably wait until the afternoon. I've got to do a few things this morning but in the afternoon I'm free and I can take you for a tour of the surf park myself."

"Cool. In the meanwhile, I can, hurrr, read about marine biology."

Clayton looked at me. He was calculating something. Then he said, "You know what, read whatever you want. I don't care. Just read everything in here; don't take any books from the library. Deal?"

"Deal."

And with that, Clayton left.

Maybe Clayton wasn't such a bad guy after all. Maybe I had been conflating too many weird coincidences into some sort of conspiracy theory that really wasn't there. As my science teacher says, "Correlation is not causation ... but it might be."

The squid and the bunny with red eyes could be explained with a trick of the light or maybe some sort of contaminant. The sightings of Herobrine and Entity 303 could be explained by hallucinations caused by anger or fear. Even Claire's hallucination of a witch could be explained because she was so tired as well as angry at me. Maybe.

Still, that horrible vibe I got from Clayton was still concerning me.

I decided to put the marine biology books back and return to the occult section.

Day 26 – Afternoon

I'd spent the morning reading through the various occult books in the library which might contain something that would explain what I had seen and experienced.

I could now confirm that there were villagers in the past who had learned how to use evoking skills and possess passive mobs and even other villagers and players. According to the books, it was quite difficult to learn these skills, but they could be learned. It was very dangerous and could cause injury or death to the target of the novice Evoker or even to the novice him or herself.

The books warned that pursuing a path of evoking and possession was likely to draw the ire of the most powerful beings in the mythology of Minecraft including Notch, Herobrine, and Entity 303.

So, I thought, if Clayton was using evoking, maybe the reason Herobrine and Entity 303 had appeared was because they were upset at him using evoking powers?

This was all rank speculation. I could create a great conspiracy theory but I could prove nothing. Imagine presenting this evidence in a court of law. What would the evidence be? My vibes and some speculation based on a 400-year-old book? I'd be laughed out of court.

Still, it was an interesting theory and I would remain vigilant. But now the sun was hitting high noon and the servants were calling us to have lunch. I went in to have lunch with Claire, Clayton, Biff, Biff's parents, and Mr. and Mrs. Dretsky.

Mr. and Mrs. Dretsky introduced themselves to me and Biff, but Biff's parents knew them from way back.

They seemed like nice enough people. They were both very generous and told great stories while we ate lunch. Mrs. Dretsky was fashionably dressed and very thin. She wore lots of makeup and earrings and had all kinds of weird shiny glittery doodads in her hair. Mr. Dretsky was tall and muscular, looking 10 years younger than his stated age of 50.

"So, Jimmy, Clayton tells me you boys are going to go ride the surf park this afternoon," said Mr. Dretsky.

"Yes, sir. I'd like to see it. Maybe I can get some ideas for how to modify my own surf park."

"I have a SUP park," said Biff, not wanting to be left out.

"One of these days, I might have to try this surfing or SUPing," said Mr. Dretsky. "Unfortunately, my business ventures keep me far too busy at this time. Maybe in a few weeks."

"Oh, dear, you need to relax a bit more. You're going to stress yourself into an early puff of smoke," said Mrs. Dretsky with a worried voice.

Mr. Dretsky laughed. "I'm not planning on turning into a puff of smoke anytime soon, honey. I'm just really busy right now."

Mrs. Dretsky looked at me and rolled her eyes, showing her disbelief. "Well, hurrr, whatever."

The conversation went on like that for another half an hour as we ate delicious sandwiches and drank fruit juice.

Once lunch was done and the servants had cleared everything away, Clayton, Biff, and I put on bathing suits, pulled our robes over them, and walked to the surf park.

* * *

We arrived at the surf park a few minutes later. As we walked in, I noticed just about everybody had on multicolored bathing suits. I was wearing my plain blue bathing suit. There were only a few others dressed as simply as I was, including Biff who was wearing a purple bathing suit. At least I had a multicolored robe on over the bathing suit, so I didn't feel entirely like a Capitol City noob.

When we walked in, everyone noticed Clayton was in our group. They all stared at him, amazed. As we walked through the crowd, some of the villagers said, "Thanks for making the surf park. It's awesome." Some girls said, "You're so cute."

Clayton laughed. "Jimmy, Biff, let's get to the changing room and get out there. One guy can only take so much adoration."

I had a feeling Clayton could endure more adoration than most.

We walked over to the changing room and I took off my robe and hung it in a closet. Clayton and Biff hung their robes too. After that, Clayton opened a locked door where he had his personal stash of surfboards. "Take any one you like," he said.

I found one with three fins on it, a "thruster" as surfers called it. It looked like it would be a good board.

229

Clayton grabbed a similar board and Biff, who had never learned how to surf, went with a SUP.

After selecting our boards, Clayton led us to another door which opened on to a private pier that went out into the water!

"See, I just walk out of the door and then I jump into the middle of the water and choose which wave I want to ride," said Clayton proudly.

Looking out from the door, I could not believe the size of the surf park. First of all, it was indoors in the middle of a city, not in the ocean. Somehow, Clayton had built a structure larger than I'd ever seen and then pumped all this water into this giant building.

The surf park had three different wave making mechanisms, each pushing a different direction. One went over some sort of underwater surface that made a giant barreling wave, similar to what was at my surf park. Another mechanism made a mushy, weak wave that was suitable for beginners. The third wave broke a long distance without a barrel but with a steep wave face that allowed deep bottom turns and aggressive top turns and cutbacks. Surfers called it a "point break"-style wave.

"Holy Notch, this is amazing," I couldn't help but say.

Clayton smiled and then jumped into the water. He yelled back, "Let's get pitted!"

We spent the rest of the afternoon riding the different waves. Biff even stroked his SUP into a few of the mushy waves and after about an hour, went back inside and got a smaller surfboard and actually seemed to be having fun without a paddle.

Clayton was ripping even harder than he did when he was at my surf park. I had to say he might be the best surfer I'd ever seen.

Well, almost the best. After we been surfing for over an hour, I saw someone paddling out who I thought I recognized. When he got closer, I saw that it was Laird. *He* was the best surfer I'd ever seen.

"Jimmy, what's up? I was hoping I'd see you here," said Laird with a big smile on his face.

"Laird! Good to see you. Clayton was just letting me check out his surf park."

Laird sat up on his board and said, "Hey, Clayton, this place is awesome. It's almost like surfing in the real world where I'm from."

I couldn't believe it, but Clayton was actually blushing a little bit. "Thanks, man. That means a lot coming from a player who actually surfs on real waves that were not made by machines."

Laird continued. "I'm just glad Jimmy and Emma figured out how to do it in the first place. Your park is totally awesome, but you have to admit, without Jimmy and Emma, this place wouldn't exist."

After Laird dispensed his wisdom, he turned around and paddled into a giant barrel and got spat out. Instead of paddling back out to where we were, he paddled over to the take off spot for the point break.

I looked over Clayton. I was still picking up an evil vibe, but it didn't seem quite as strong as before. Maybe being in the water was reducing his evilness, or perhaps the water was just interfering with my ability to pick up his evil vibes.

Anyway, we were having a good time surfing. I didn't want to think about his evilness while I was out here in the water. I didn't want to destroy the purity of my surfing stoke.

We surfed for about another hour before we paddled back to the private pier and climbed up a ladder that was monitored by a security guard.

"Welcome back to land, sir," said the security guard, who was one of the most muscular villagers I had ever seen. He was so buff that he seemed as though he had been genetically altered.

"Thanks, Nick, glad to be back," said Clayton in a paternalistic tone.

I shook my head. How weird it must be to be this rich and have all these people fawning over you.

Anyway, we walked back inside the changing room, dried off, and put our robes back on. Biff was already in there waiting for us, having left the water about fifteen minutes earlier.

"So, what should we do now?" asked Biff.

"Well, I have a few business items to take care of," said Clayton. "Why don't you and Jimmy go back to the house and I'll be back in time for dinner."

"Sounds like a plan," I said.

Day 26 – Evening

Everyone was gathered around the dinner table, Clayton's parents, Clayton, Claire, Biff, Biff's parents, and me. As with previous meals, there was an overabundance of food on the table and numerous servants standing around waiting to serve it to us.

During dinner, I tried to get some more information about the Dretsky business empire. I was hoping to find some sort of evidence that might link it to the possessions and the evoking I suspected enabled the possessions.

"So, Mr. Dretsky, I've heard that your family imports raw materials from the Nether. What do you do with them?" I asked.

Mr. Dretsky finished chewing the food in his mouth and swallowed. He put his fork down on the edge of his plate and then said, "The Dretsky family has found a market for mainly netherrack in the Overworld. When netherrack is converted to nether brick, it becomes a very strong building material. It is used extensively in the multistory buildings in Capitol City for extra strong foundations and structural support. Netherrack is the main raw material we bring into the Overworld. It is very lucrative."

I nodded my understanding. "So, do you trade with the Nether mobs then? Like, are the zombie pigmen running the place, or what?"

I noticed out of the corner of my eye that Clayton was looking at me curiously. It was like he was beginning to worry that I was pressing all the wrong buttons. I glanced at Claire to see if she was exhibiting any of the same concern. It didn't appear that she was. She was simply eating her food and waiting for the next person to talk.

"Jimmy, our negotiations with the Nether mobs are quite complicated. The zombie pigmen do have quite a bit of control down there, but the blazes and ghasts are also extremely important to keep happy. After all, the only way to get ghast tears is to either kill them or to have them collect the tears for you. Killing takes a lot of effort so we prefer to have good relations with the ghasts."

Did he just imply that he would be willing to kill ghasts for their tears? I think he did.

"Oh, okay," I said. "So do the mobs, like, have governments and leaders or do you have to negotiate with individual groups?"

Clayton put up his hand. "I'll take this one, Father."

Clayton turned around and looked at me. He steepled his hands in front of his face and silently judged me for a couple of seconds. It was uncomfortable. Then he began. "A long time ago, before I was born, that is what the Dretsky family had to do, negotiate with individual groups. However, since we've been conducting business with the Nether mobs, they have formed themselves into governments, partly to get better deals from us and partly because I think they realize that working together is better than working separately. In fact, that's why I was in the Nether the other day when you arrived. I was negotiating a new trade agreement with the magma cube government officials."

Biff choked on his food and coughed a couple times and then said, "The magma cubes have a government?"

Clayton nodded. "It is a rather dysfunctional government, jumping rapidly between different ideas, but it is a government nonetheless."

"What sort of materials do you import from the magma cubes?" asked Biff.

"You know how magma cubes hop around a lot? Well, they provide us with the ingredients for the propulsion system inside their bodies. We are starting to develop applications in the construction and transportation industries. It's all new as of yet, but our scientists are working on it feverishly."

This is really amazing, I thought. I had no idea that you could do such things. No wonder the Dretskys were billionaires.

"It must be pretty cool to visit the Nether so often," I said.

I saw Clayton's eyes squint a little bit and then he began to slowly nod. I was starting to feel the evil vibes coming back. Then Clayton said, "You want to visit the Nether? I could take you."

At that point Biff's father said, "Hold on now, Clayton, Jimmy is here under my protection and I gave his parents my word that I wouldn't let him do anything dangerous. I know you go to the Nether all the time, but I still think it's too dangerous for him to go. I won't allow it."

Mr. Dretsky chimed in, "Oh come now, the Nether is not very dangerous. We can send them down there was some bodyguards if it'll make you feel better. It's really not a big deal."

Biff's father shook his head. "I cannot allow that. That is a decision for Jimmy's parents, and they are not here to make it."

"Oh, come on," I whined. "I want to go. Please? Hurrr. Please?"

"Sorry, Jimmy, if your parents were here, they could make that decision, but they aren't. Unfortunately, there exists no technology in the Overworld that would allow me to contact them from this great distance and get their approval. Therefore, I have to say no," said Biff's father.

I sighed. "I understand." I poked at my food with my fork.

The rest of the meal was filled with small talk about business dealings and the weather. I didn't pay attention. I really did want to go to the Nether, even if it was with a jerk like Clayton. I really wanted to be able to tell my friends I'd been down there. Especially Emma, she would be so jealous.

After dinner, we returned to our rooms and packed our belongings because we were going to be leaving the next day around 9:00 in the morning. We would be retracing our route to Creeper Junction and then to Zombie Bane.

After I finished packing, I fell asleep quickly, and yet again, had no dreams.

Day 27 – Morning

The sun had not yet come up when I felt someone shaking my shoulder. I slowly woke up and looked over and saw Clayton standing above me. He had his finger to his lips indicating I should be quiet. He handed me my robe and motioned that I should come with him.

I got up, put on my robe, and followed Clayton. We went down the hallway a bit and then entered another room. When we got inside, Clayton shut the door and ignited a torch so we could see.

"Do you really want to see the Nether?" asked Clayton.

"Well, I do, but after what Biff's dad said, I don't think I should really go."

"What are you, a baby? It's no big deal."

"I don't know, we have to leave pretty soon and I don't want to get in trouble."

Clayton shook his head and laughed. "Come on. Don't you want to tell your girlfriend Emma all about it?"

I felt my face flushing both with embarrassment and anger. "She's not my girlfriend!"

"Jimmy, you will always be a loser in Zombie Bane. You need to see what else is out there. The Nether will blow your mind."

I had no doubt it would blow my mind. I probably shouldn't have agreed to go, but I did. It was too easy. Clayton was right there. No one would know I was gone. We might even get back before they woke up.

"Okay, Clayton. But let's just go for like half an hour. I really don't want Biff's parents to find out I'm gone."

Clayton smiled. "Okay. No worries, mate. Just a quick trip."

Clayton led me out of the room and down the hall where, after a series of twists and turns, we arrived at another door. Clayton opened the door and a strange purple glow came through the crack of the door as he slowly opened it.

We walked into the room and I saw an active nether portal.

"Wow! I've never seen a nether portal before. Not in person anyway, just in drawings." I said.

"Pretty cool, isn't it?"

"It sure is, Clayton. So, what do we do now?"

"It's easy. We just walk up to the portal and step in. We will pop out on the other side in the Nether, and then we can walk around and I'll show you a couple things and then we will be back before anyone knows it."

"Sounds awesome."

Clayton led the way to the nether portal and stood in front of it. He looked at me and said, "Just walk like you normally walk. You won't feel a thing. One moment you'll be in this room, and the next you'll be in the Nether." And with that, he walked into the nether portal and disappeared.

I could feel my heart racing and my breath increasing in speed. I felt like I was going to pass out. I cautiously slowed my breathing and, when I felt a little bit more under control, I stepped into the nether portal. With my next step ... I was inside a red-hued world that was hot and humid and smelly. And Clayton was standing right next to me.

"I ... I ... can't believe it," I said in awe.

"Cool, right? Come on, let's look around."

For the next fifteen minutes, Clayton showed me around the area near the nether portal. We encountered some magma cubes who said "Hi" to Clayton. We saw a few ghasts floating at a distance inside a large cavern. A blaze passed by and waved its flaming hand in acknowledgment to Clayton. We even talked with a group of zombie pigmen, who said that all business operations were well under control.

"Wow, Clayton, all these hostile mobs aren't hostile to you at all. Your family has really done a good job negotiating agreements with them."

Clayton nodded. "It's true. Although, I have to admit that I'm the one who's really made the relationships blossom in the past couple of years. Before that, there was always some hostility underneath each group of mobs, but now, they genuinely like working with us."

"Why is that? What of you been doing differently?"

Clayton grinned like a wolf, an evil wolf. "Trade secret. If I told you, I'd have to kill you."

I laughed, but it didn't really seem like Clayton was joking.

"Plus, I've had some additional assistance in convincing the natives to become more ... hurr, what is the right word? Compliant," Clayton said in a sinister tone.

I was about to ask him what he meant when from behind a nearby rock stepped an Evoker!

In fact, I recognized him. He was the Evoker from the wanted poster at the police station in Zombie Bane!

"I knew you were working with an Evoker!" I yelled. "I knew I should've trusted the evil vibes I was picking up from you!"

Clayton laughed at me. "And now, it's too late."

I got a horrible sinking feeling in the pit of my stomach. Is Clayton going to kill me? Or would the Evoker do it for him?

It was time for action, not words. I turned and ran as fast as I could toward the nether portal. I thought that if I could get through it, I could run to Biff's family and they could protect me. I didn't think Clayton would try to do anything in front of them.

As I sprinted away, I heard Clayton yell, "Get him!"

I didn't bother looking back. I knew the Evoker was after me because I could hear his footsteps. I hoped I could outrun him and his spells, but then in front of me four zombie pigmen suddenly jumped out from behind some rocks and blocked my path. I skidded to a halt.

I looked left and right and saw a small opening to the left. I sprinted for the opening but then suddenly a blaze appeared in it blocking my way.

I was trapped.

I heard a slow clapping sound and turned to see Clayton walking towards me slowly applauding.

"Nice try, Jimmy, but you are the pathetic loser in this story, and I'm the rich and famous winner. You'll never get away."

I started shivering. Was this it? Was I about to become a puff of smoke and respawn somewhere else, with a new family, with a new life where I didn't know anything about surfing? I could feel a tear forming in my right eye but I willed myself to stay strong in front of Clayton and the tear tried up.

"Are you going to kill me now?"

Clayton laughed again. "Why would I kill you?"

I don't believe this, was he going to let me go? I was feeling the most evil vibes coming from him that I'd felt ever, but he seemed like he was going to let me live. *What was his plan?*

"Of course I'm not going to kill you, I'm going to make you work for me. That's what I do to all of my enemies."

"Enemies? How am I your enemy? I thought we were going to work together with the Surf Park advertising," I said, completely confused.

Clayton sighed and shook his head. "See, this is why I'm a billionaire and you are a pathetic loser. *Anyone* who makes money is my enemy. My goal is to create a world where the only person who makes money is me."

I was astonished by Clayton's next-level greed. I looked into his eyes and saw that he was sincere in his belief that he wanted to create a world where no one but himself could make money.

"You're insane!" I yelled.

Clayton shrugged. "Maybe I am, but I'm rich. That's all that matters."

I saw Clayton move his hand, indicating something. At that moment the four zombie pigmen standing around me grabbed my arms, restraining me.

"You can't do this Clayton. Biff and his family and my parents will come looking for me. You won't get away with this."

Clayton sighed and shook his head again, indicating that I was stupid. "Really? I think what happened was Jimmy got up early and started looking around the house. We found his multicolored robe next to the nether portal. He must've gone exploring down there and gotten lost. We sent a search party, but couldn't find him. I'm sorry, but he is lost forever. Probably – *tear, sniff* – dead."

My jaw fell open. Clayton was going to pretend that I got myself killed by doing something stupid. And, he was such a good actor, he was going to succeed.

"No! You can't do this to me!" I yelled. Tears were finally starting to stream down my face. I couldn't restrain myself anymore. I knew this was the end.

"Take him from my sight," Clayton said to the zombie pigmen.

As I was led away the Evoker stared at me wordlessly. I saw him twitch his finger slightly and Herobrine and Entity 303 appeared in front of me. They did a little dance and then disappeared. I looked over at the Evoker. He grinned at me knowingly.

"It was you. You made me see those things," I said.

The Evoker narrowed his eyes and nodded without saying a word.

I'd been led down this path the entire time. Clayton had been thinking about capturing me ever since he laid eyes on the Surf 'n Snack. And now he had succeeded. My only solace was that Emma was still free and operating the Surf 'n Snack. But, if Clayton had done this to get me, he would probably do the same thing to Emma.

I felt so helpless.

The zombie pigmen led me down a narrow corridor and then into a larger room and finally to a door. They opened the door and shoved me and then locked the door behind me.

Inside the room I saw dozens of villagers in various states of degradation. Some looked like they had just been captured and others looked like they'd been there for months, maybe years.

They looked at me with forlorn eyes but said nothing. We knew we were trapped.

I sat down on the ground and started to cry.

"Stop crying, Jimmy. We're going to get out of this," said a confident female voice.

I looked up and standing in front of me was Emma!

I wiped my tears and then stood up and hugged her. *Yes, it is true, I hugged her.* "How? Hurr. How did he get you?"

"The Evoker. I was walking home after closing the Surf 'n Snack yesterday and the Evoker hypnotized me somehow. I woke up in a building somewhere in Zombie Bane surrounded by zombie pigmen. When I woke up, they escorted me through a nether portal and brought me here."

"I'm so sorry this happened to you, Emma."

She shook her head. "It's not your fault. Besides, I told you. We're going to get out of here. And, then, we are going to get our revenge on Clayton."

END of Book 4

DIARY OF A SURFER VILLAGER

SURFER

VILLAGER

Book 5

(an unofficial Minecraft book)

Day 28 – Morning

I slept fitfully during the night. The ground in our jail was hard and the zombie pigmen did not provide us with any pillows or blankets. I had pulled my robe around me tightly in an attempt to retain some body heat, but it didn't work. I shivered all night long.

It was the most miserable night of my life.

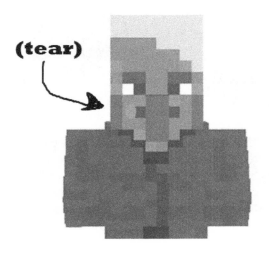

(tear)

Now, this morning, one of the zombie pigmen threw open the door to the room and yelled at us to wake up. "Come on, slaves! Get up you lazy animals!"

Three more zombie pigmen followed him into the room, each with a golden sword in one hand and a stick in the other. There was menace in their eyes.

I wiped the sleep from my eyes and was just starting to stand up when one of the zombie pigmen came by and hit me with a stick. "Faster, slave! When I say jump, you say how high."

"Ouch," I said rubbing my arm where he had hit me. "I'm no magma cube, man. I can only jump a few inches."

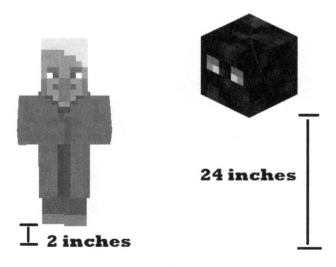

2 inches

24 inches

The zombie pigman gave me a startled look. Was he surprised that I had talked back? Or was he in awe of the awesome joke I had just made? I'll probably never know because his simplistic response was to hit me again with the wooden stick, this time on my leg.

"Okay, slaves. Form a line at the door. You have five seconds."

Everyone rushed to the door to get in line. I made sure I was standing with Emma, behind her, actually. Behind me was a decrepit old villager man who looked like he wouldn't live more than a few days. In front of Emma was a villager woman who looked like she hadn't been in the Nether for too long; her robe was still somewhat clean.

"Get moving!" ordered one of the zombie pigmen, cracking his stick against the cold, hard ground for emphasis.

We followed one of the guards through several passageways for several minutes before we came to a chamber where netherrack mining was in progress. There was a pile of iron pickaxes in the center of the room.

The villagers who had been in captivity longer than me, robotically walked to the pile of pickaxes and grabbed one. I followed Emma to the pile and we each selected a pickaxe.

"Get to work!" shouted one of the guards as he slammed his wooden stick against the ground. The crisp crack of the wood hitting the hard rock echoed sharply off the walls of the chamber. All this stick cracking was giving me a headache.

Emma and I walked over to one side of the chamber and began mining. We mined for about twenty minutes, methodically moving our arms up and down like human pumpjacks. We quickly assembled a substantial pile of netherrack blocks behind us.

About every ten minutes, a zombie pigman passed by with a couple of villager slaves dragging a cart. They would load the netherrack blocks in the cart and drag it away.

When no guards were nearby, Emma said, "I hate this place. I can't believe how evil Clayton is to force his own kind into slavery."

I brought the point of the pickaxe down against the wall. My hands were beginning to hurt. "Yeah, it's hard to believe he's not even an adult yet and he is already so evil. I'm surprised he doesn't have glowing red eyes!"

Emma nodded. In between strokes of the pickaxe, she said, "You know, yesterday when I was walking through the passageways back to our jail after our workday was over, I overheard an Evoker talking to some unknown figure. The two of them were talking about some sort of religious ritual, involving ancient creepers or something? I thought I heard something about attaining additional power or unspeakable power. Something like that."

I tensed when I heard this. "Have you heard about the rainbow creeper religion?"

"No, I haven't," said Emma with a curious look on her face.

"When we were traveling to Capitol City, Biff's dad mentioned it was some sort of ancient sect that had broken away from the worship of Notch. They worshiped creepers and were banished into the wasteland before founding the village of Creeper Junction. Biff's dad seemed to think the religion was nearly defunct and only had a few adherents remaining. But, maybe that's not the case?"

Emma nodded her head in thought. "I wish we could do some research about that religion. I've never heard of it before. For all I know it claims to offer some path to unlimited power. I can see why some people would want to try and get that."

I winced with pain as I lifted my pickaxe and brought it down against the wall for the 723rd time today. (Yeah, I'd been keeping count.) "I can't believe we've only been picking away for less than an hour. I'm going to be so sore tonight."

Emma laughed. "I thought you would have been in shape from all that surfing you've been doing."

"I probably should be, but surfing uses different muscles than mining. Anyway, the fact that you heard someone talking about rainbow creepers and that I've recently learned about rainbow creepers is concerning.

It feels like something is going on that we don't fully comprehend."

At that moment I had a terrible memory. The blood drained from my face. I probably looked more like husk villager than a normal villager.

Emma noticed. "Oh my Notch! What is it Jimmy?"

I sighed heavily. "I just remembered. One day Claire was wearing a new brown robe with a really small rainbow creeper logo on it. She said it was just some sort a new fashion brand, but ... what if it's more? What if she's a member of the religion and is planning some sort of evil?!?"

Emma clicked her tongue and squinted her eyes. "I suppose it could be either one of those things. Leave it to some greedy idiots in Capitol City to engage in religious cultural appropriation for the sake of fashion."

At that moment a zombie pigman came up and hit us both with a stick. "No talking. Working only. Girl, you over there," said the zombie pigman as he pointed to the other side of the chamber.

I could tell Emma was extremely upset at being told what to do and wanted to say something to the zombie pigman. But she was too smart for that. Instead, she just shouldered her pickaxe and walked silently across the room.

The zombie pigman turned to me and said, "Boy, if I see you talking to anyone else today, I'll beat you so hard you can't even walk."

"Brah, chill. I'm easy like Sunday morning. I'm just going to be picking away for the rest of the day. I ain't gonna play, so you don't have to flay. Cool?"

The zombie pigman was so taken aback by my awesome rap that he just shook his head and backed away. If I didn't know any better, I would've said he was afraid of me.

Skills.

As I returned to the repetitive monotony of mining, my mind began to wander. I wondered about the rainbow creeper religion. I wondered about Claire's robe. I wondered if Clayton was some sort of leader in the religion or if maybe it was his father or maybe it was an Evoker who was their ally.

I realized I was completely speculating without any basis in fact and so I stopped. It was then that I remembered Biff and his parents would probably be arriving in Zombie Bane tomorrow. If we couldn't get out of here, he would tell my parents I was dead. That made me sad.

* * *

After we completed our morning's work, the zombie pigmen gave us a generous fifteen-minute break. They tossed each of us an apple. We ate in silence, the crunching of our teeth into the flesh of the apples

257

echoing against the walls of the chamber were the only sounds heard.

When the lunch break was over, we went back to work for another five hours.

* * *

When the afternoon shift was done, I put my pickaxe back in the pile the center of the room. My hands were blistered and bleeding. We formed up the line and walked back to the room where we were imprisoned.

As the zombie pigman guard began to close the door and lock us in for the night, he said, "Don't get any stupid ideas in there, slaves. You will never escape. Someone will stop by soon with your dinner. Tonight it's pork chops, and they're only slightly rotten."

I could hear the zombie pigman laughing to himself as he shut the door and locked it.

Emma walked over and sat next to me against the wall. I felt like crying until Emma whispered, "I think I know a way we can escape. But we will have to wait until tomorrow."

Day 29 – Morning

Last night after "dinner," which consisted of cold rotten pork chops, Emma told me her plan for escape. It was the most disgusting thing I've ever eaten in my life ... the dinner, not Emma's plan.

Obviously, one cannot eat a "plan" because a "plan" is just a bunch of words. I suppose one could eat a plan if it were written on paper, but then one would be eating paper more than eating the plan, *n'est-ce pas*? It was a conundrum I did not have time to decipher.

I could tell you what Emma's plan was right now, but that would violate the rules of diary writing and writing in general. The main rule of writing is to "show not tell." So, rather than telling you the plan in advance so you're not surprised as you read on in this diary, I will not tell you the plan at all. Instead you'll have to live through it with me every step of the way.

Will we escape? Or will we be captured? Or worse? You'll have to read in order to discover the answers to these profound questions.

I thought Emma's plan was risky, but I thought it might work as well. Either way, I didn't want to go back to the netherrack mine for another horrible monotonous day of hitting my pickaxe against the wall.

We villagers are not very strong and have little endurance when it comes to mining activities. We prefer to make our money by trading goods or selling things, rather than pulling things out of the ground. Of course, Clayton and his family had made their fortune by doing exactly that: pulling things out of the ground. So, maybe my view of what it means to be a villager is all messed up. I'll have to think about that someday, if I manage to escape.

Anyway...

One of the zombie pigmen came into the room where we slept and yelled at us to get up. Another zombie pigman threw an apple to each of us for breakfast. Emma and I pretended to eat our apples but instead we tucked them into our inventories. The apples were part of the plan.

"Now that you've had your delicious and nutritious breakfast, get moving!" yelled one of the zombie pigmen.

We stood up and formed a line like we had the other day. I made sure to get in line behind Emma, per the plan. Unfortunately, I had elbow an elderly villager out of the way. He'd been standing behind Emma for a few seconds by the time I got there. As I worked my way in front of him, he said "Hey, no cut-sies!"

I looked at the old man with shame in my eyes. If we'd been outside of this prison cell, I never would've done this, but this was part of the escape plan. Some of the shame in my eyes was also because I knew that I wasn't going to be taking this man, or anyone else, with me when I escaped. Maybe I'd return some day to rescue everyone, but not today.

"Sorry, sir, I need to stand here."

The old villager rolled his eyes. "What? Is she your girlfriend?"

I huffed and puffed with anger. My rage and embarrassment showed plainly on my face. "She's not my girlfriend. She's just ... she's ... well, she's my friend and she's a girl, so if that means she's my girlfriend, then, yes, she's my girlfriend. But, if you meant, like, do we hold hands and stuff, then no, she's not my girlfriend."

Emma giggled as I tried to explain why I needed to cut in line. The old man shook his head and muttered something about stupid kids.

One of the pigmen noticed the commotion and came over. "What's going on here, slave?"

I looked at the pigman, I was very concerned. If I couldn't be directly behind Emma, our plan might not work. "Um, I just wanted to get in line behind Emma."

The pigman growled. "Slaves don't have names." He paused for a minute and then, with a sly grin, asked, "What? Is she your girlfriend or something?"

I slapped my forehead. I shook my head from side to side. I shrugged my shoulders a few times. I let my head fall until my chin touched my chest. I looked like a deflated question mark. "No, she is *not* my girlfriend."

The zombie pigman growled again. "I don't want to see you misbehaving at all today or you won't get any mushroom stew for dinner."

"Yes, sir. I understand," I said, while secretly smiling to myself. I already knew I wasn't going to have mushroom stew at all today. I was going to escape. And if I didn't escape, then I'd be punished by not having mushroom stew, so it was TRUTH that I wasn't going to have mushroom stew. So, in a life full of uncertainties, that was one certainty that I carried with me for the rest of the morning. It felt good to be certain about something.

As we left the room, there was a pigman at the front of the line, and one at the end of the line with the other two moving back and forth up and down the sides of the line. There were about twenty or so of us slaves.

We began walking through the various corridors again to get to the mining site. Walking in front of Emma was a young villager who I had not noticed the other day. He turned around and whispered, "This is so lame."

Emma and I nodded. "Where are you from?" I asked.

"Capitol City," he said quietly. "My name's Noah."

"Emma and Jimmy," said Emma.

A zombie pigman noticed our conversation and came up to us and hit each of us with his wooden stick. "Silence, slaves!" We complied, walking in silence.

When we got to one particular T-shaped intersection, the line turned right. Immediately after Noah had turned right, Emma got to the intersection and should have turned right, but instead, she yelled, "Now!" We both dashed to the left.

Emma got away, but a zombie pigman was too quick, dove after me, and grabbed my leg! I tried to pull it away, but could not free myself. Emma turned around and looked at me, desperation in her eyes.

"Just go," I yelled, resigning myself to a beating followed by a sort, miserable life of slavery in the Nether.

But then, suddenly, my leg was free and I was running. I looked back and saw that Noah had jumped on the zombie pigman's arm, forcing him to let go of my leg.

"Run, Jimmy, run!" yelled Noah.

"Come with us!" I shouted back. But, before Noah could answer, a zombie pigman stepped in front of him, blocking his path.

I knew I couldn't help him so I turned back around and ran as fast as I could after Emma. I looked over my shoulder and saw that two of the four zombie pigman guards were pursuing us.

We opened up a good lead on the surprised pigmen, but we could still hear their footsteps behind us echoing on the walls of the corridors through which we ran.

"Come back here, slaves!" they yelled. Only two pigmen pursued us because the other two had to guard the prisoners who had remained. I imagined the looks on the faces of the prisoners, including brave Noah who we had just met, but who had saved us. I'm sure they were shocked. Some were jealous. Some were angry. Some were probably crying. Some were disappointed that we hadn't shared our plan with them. They probably knew that because of our currently successful escape attempt, the guards would be increased and their own chances of ever getting away would be decreased.

Sometimes, life is lame.

Emma led the way. She made assured choices of when and where to turn. I trusted her and did what she did.

Left.

Right.

Left.

Straight.

But still the pigmen followed.

"Do you know where you're going?" I asked as I ran behind her.

"I hope so."

Now, when Emma had told me her plan, she told me she *knew* where to go. My concern about being in these corridors was that we would be trapped in some sort of maze. Of course, if we had mining equipment, we might be able to dig a way out. We could find a back way to get to a nether portal and return to the Overworld. But if we just ran around deeper and deeper into the mine, eventually we would either meet a dead end and be captured or we would be so irretrievably lost that we would starve to death. Had I known this, I might not have agreed to the plan, but it was now too late.

When we came to a narrow part of the path, the pigmen had started to gain on us. But that was when Emma yelled, "Apples! Now!"

We both reached into our inventories and pulled out our rotten apples and dropped them on the ground behind us and continued running.

The pigmen were closing on us but they didn't see the apples. The first pigman stepped on the apple. It squished under his foot and created a low friction surface which caused him to slip, slide and then fall and hit his head on the ground, knocking him out.

The other pigman saw the apple and avoided it but couldn't avoid his fallen comrade and tripped over him and fell to the ground with a crash. "I'll get you for this, you meddling kids!" yelled the fallen, but still conscious, zombie pigman.

I laughed with triumph. "It worked!"

Emma, who was still running in front of me, turned around and said, "Yeah, I'm pretty smart, right?"

"So far so good," I said, giving her a thumbs up followed by a shaka.

I knew that the zombie pigmen would not stop chasing us, but we had opened up a large gap between them. Probably at least ten seconds between the pigman who was still conscious, and who knows how long that it would take for the other pigman to regain consciousness.

We kept running for another few minutes until we arrived at a door and stopped.

"I think this is the door," said Emma.

"How did you know this was here?"

"I noticed there was a pattern to the mining operation. I assumed that the path we took would follow that same pattern. I calculated the turns it would take to arrive at this location, which I assumed would be the door to a nether portal room. I hope I'm right."

I was completely flabbergasted. If Emma had been able to calculate this in her brain, she must be some sort of genius. I knew she was highly skilled with mechanisms and contraptions and science, but now it seemed like she was some sort of mathematical savant, hiding behind her shy exterior. Don't judge a book by its cover kids, don't judge a book.

"You are like some sort of Maze Runner, or Ms. Pac-Man, or something," I said.

"Huh?"

"Never mind."

We crouched behind a rock, just in case the door opened, so we would not be seen.

"Okay, so, the nether portal to Zombie Bane should be behind that door," whispered Emma. "I'm pretty sure. This feels familiar."

"Feels?"

"I was blindfolded when they transported me from Zombie Bane to the Nether."

"I hope you are right. Let's do this thing," I said triumphantly, but then realized I had no idea what to do. I scratched my head and said sheepishly, "So, what do we do now?"

"I think there should be two zombie pigmen in there, but no more. So, basically, we just need to rush in and jump into the nether portal no matter what."

I nodded my head. "Let's go."

At that moment, we heard the footsteps of the zombie pigman pursuer running behind us. It was now or never. I looked at Emma. She looked at me. Our eyes met. It was go time.

We both jumped up and opened the door.

When we entered the room, we saw one zombie pigman leaning against the wall biting his nails. The other zombie pigman was standing near the nether portal twirling a spear in his left hand. We were almost to the nether portal before they even noticed us. The one biting his nails looked up, spit a giant fingernail out of his mouth and said to his colleague, "Stop them, Mateo!"

Mateo the pigman stopped twirling his spear when we were just a few steps from the nether portal. "I got this, David," he yelled to the other pigman.

Mateo grabbed hold of his spear with both his hands. He took a strong stance and then thrust the spear in front of another portal, intending to block our path.

But. Nothing. Was. Going. To. Stop. Us. Today.

I slid on my knees and leaned back like I was doing the limbo and began to slide underneath the spear. Emma did a handspring and propelled herself into the air, spinning backward over the spear. I looked over at Mateo and winked.

As we passed into the nether portal, we heard David yell, "Oh geez, man, ah shucks!"

Day 29 – Morning, continued

So, I could've kept telling the story of the escape in the prior journal entry, but it seemed like it was getting kind of long. I know some people just like to read one chapter at a time or one journal entry at a time, so I thought I would stop it there for a moment. Ending a journal entry with jumping through a portal seems like a logical place, don't you agree?

Anyway....

So, less than one second after we had entered the nether portal, we popped out the other side into a room filled with old books on rickety wooden shelves. We landed on the floor with a thud. Or, maybe it was more like a bump. Or, some combination of the two, like a thuddy thud bump bumpity bumpy thud.

I looked around and was confused by the fact that we were in a room filled with books. "This was the nether portal the pigmen brought you to when they captured you in Zombie Bane?" I asked Emma.

Emma brushed the dust and dirt off of her robe. She looked around and nodded. "Yeah, this is it."

"Are we ... hurrr ... in the library?" I asked.

"I think so," said Emma. "Probably in its basement. No one ever comes down here."

It was then that I noticed there were several other nether portals in the room! I was about to ask Emma if she knew anything about the other portals when we heard footsteps coming. Before we could hide, two zombie pigmen and the librarian [!!!!!] came around the corner.

"What?!? You? You're in league with Clayton?!?" I shouted at the librarian.

The librarian laughed, or more properly she cackled. "You stupid kids. You believed all that stuff about me not allowing occult filth in the library? I *live* for the occult."

I'm not quite sure what it means to "live for the occult," but I knew the librarian was evil. That's all I needed to know.

At that moment, the librarian yelled to the two zombie pigmen, "Get them!"

Emma grabbed my arm and started to run the opposite direction. I did not have time to think; I just reacted. I followed her.

As the two zombie pigmen pursued us, one of them yelled at the other, "Go tell master Clayton we've located them. I'll try to stop them."

The zombie pigman jumped into one of the other nether portals in the room. His act seemed to answer my question about the purpose of the other nether portals.

This room must be a transportation hub for Clayton's forces. The nether portal Emma and I came through went to the mining area. The nether portal the zombie pigman jumped in must have gone to another location in the Nether, perhaps where I had entered the mining area, where he could then transfer to yet another nether portal that would lead back to the Dretsky estate.

I wondered how many places you could get if you simply knew which nether portals to use. It was an elegant solution to the slow transportation options otherwise available on the Overworld.

While I was contemplating solutions to worldwide transportation bottlenecks, the other pigman had gained on us.

"Hurry up," yelled Emma. "There's a door ahead."

I began running as fast as I could, not that I wasn't already, but somehow I found another speed that I had only dreamed of. Actually, I'd never dreamed of running very fast – I have dreamed of flying, though – but it seemed like a pretty cool thing to write.

Anyway, we were just about to the door when the zombie pigman threw a spear at us. Fortunately, his aim was off, and the spear sailed just above our heads. Unfortunately, the spear lodged in the door at a perfect angle, preventing us from opening it.

"Netherrack!" swore Emma. I'd never heard her use such foul language. But I totally agreed with her sentiment.

She turned to the left, ran to the corner of the room where a chair was resting against the wall. She stopped and picked it up and yelled, "Duck, Jimmy."

I ducked as quickly as I could and she threw the chair at the zombie pigman, hitting him in the head. The pigman was dazed, but he didn't stop coming after us. We kept running down the same passageway, but probably should have chosen a different path.

It was a dead-end.

Some fool had built a solid block column in the middle of the hallway for some reason. Maybe it was a structural element in the overall architecture of the library, designed to hold up the rooms above us. It didn't matter. It was not like I could file a complaint with the Zombie Bane Architectural Review Board.

We were trapped. The zombie pigman pulled out a golden sword and slowly came toward us.

"What will it be, kids? Do you want me to kill you, or will you surrender?"

It was an interesting question. On the one hand, we could surrender and live, but be condemned to a lifetime of mining netherrack in order to make Clayton even richer than he already was. On the other hand, we could die a valiant death in battle with our enemy and respawn somewhere else.

As I was considering my response to the pigman's question, an enderman suddenly appeared in between Emma and me and the pigman.

Emma gasped in shock. I ... well ... I'm not gonna lie, I almost peed my robe. Sweat covered my forehead and my cheeks flushed at the near disaster.

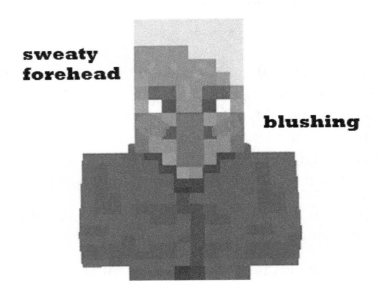

sweaty forehead

blushing

The enderman bent down and looked at us with his emotionless purple eyes and said with a strange accent – I suppose it is the accent of the End – "Come with me, if you want to live."

The pigman, having recovered from the shock of the enderman's mysterious appearance, began rushing toward the enderman ready to stab him with his golden sword.

Before Emma or I could decide our answers to the pigman's question or to the enderman's demand, the enderman wrapped his spaghetti-like black arms around us and the library vanished.

Day 29 – Continued again!

The enderman had teleported us to another room. I assumed we were still in Zombie Bane, and my suspicion was soon confirmed.

I looked around the room and saw several other endermen and an end portal. There was a window in the room which had been covered up with blocks of cobblestone in order to ensure the privacy of the occurrences inside the room. After all, villagers would freak if they knew a pack of endermen was at large in their village.

"What the heck … hurrr … is going on?" I asked, pushing the enderman's arms away.

"Forget that," said Emma. "We need to tell our parents that we're still alive."

"Yeah, and warn them not to believe anything Clayton says."

One of the endermen who had been waiting in the room came over to us. The enderman who had rescued us stood at attention and saluted.

"At ease, soldier," said the enderman standing in front of us. Our rescuer relaxed slightly, letting his arms dangle at his side.

The leader then addressed us. "You cannot speak with your parents yet. Biff and his family are, at this moment, arriving at your parents' house and informing them you disappeared. Emma's parents already believe this about her. Clayton must be convinced your parents believe you are dead, or they will be in danger too."

I was desperate. I said, "But, Clayton will know we are alive. The zombie pigman will tell him, so what's the point? We can't let our parents believe we are dead. That's cruel. They will be distraught." I felt tears starting to form in my eyes. I looked over and saw that Emma was silently sobbing too.

"Don't worry," said the leader reaching out a hand and patting each of us on the head like we were tamed wolves. "We will place a dream in your parents' minds tonight which will convince all of them that you are still alive. They will only be sad for a few hours."

"How will you do that?" asked Emma, wiping away her tears. "I've never ... hurrr ... heard of endermen doing such a thing."

"It is really quite simple if you are able to evoke. Instead of using evoking for possession and control like Clayton does, we can use it for suggestions. It is a much more elegant use of the power."

"How can you do that? Don't only illagers or evil villagers have the ability to evoke?" asked Emma.

"Endermen can't do it, but I can!" said a voice behind us. I thought I recognized it and when I turned around I couldn't believe what I was seeing.

"Mr. Blaze?!?"

"In the flesh, kids. Glad you made it back," said Mr. Blaze, still wearing the same stained robe he had on when we entered his bookshop a few days ago.

"Why didn't you tell us you have evoking powers?" said Emma. "It might've saved us some time and trouble."

Mr. Blaze looked away sheepishly. "I had no idea what you kids were after. There's a lot of strange goings-on lately. Not the least of which was when the endermen showed up in my bookshop late one night about a year ago."

I shook my head. "Wait, you and the endermen have been working together for a year? What are you working on?"

Mr. Blaze looked at the leader and raised an eyebrow, basically asking him if he could continue. The enderman gave a slight nod and then Mr. Blaze spoke. "We've been working to stop the Dretsky family, particularly Clayton. His behavior these last few years has been horrible and evil. I started hearing about it a couple years ago, when there were rumors that a villager in Capitol City was trying to gain allegiances with evildoers, including evokers, vindicators and illusioners!"

The lead enderman took over the story. "Yes, and now Clayton and his family are attempting to exploit my realm. We have encountered several villagers illegally in the End. Although we permit players to enter the End if they need to quest for the Ender Dragon, we do not permit villagers to make that trip."

I was basically lost right now. I knew there was all kinds of crazy stuff happening that was way above my pay grade, whatever that means, so I needed some clarification. "What do you mean exploiting your realm?"

The enderman sighed. It was a hollow haunting sigh, as though from an oboe or some other old-school woodwind instrument that only two dozen people in the world know how to play. "They've come for our resources. You are now painfully aware of what the Dretsky family is doing in the Nether, and in particular the enslavement of villagers so that they can get free labor to exploit the resources. They are beginning to do that in the End."

"What resources?"

The enderman sighed. "Mainly endstone and chorus flowers and fruit."

Emma squinted at the enderman. "They're not enslaving endermen are they? I don't see how they could with your teleportation abilities."

The enderman looked down at his tiny little feet, so insignificant compared to his lanky body. He paused for a moment while he contemplated his tiny little toes that he was wiggling. After he went through several different wiggling patterns – starting with the little toe and moving to the big toe then starting with the big toe and moving to the little toe and finally starting with the middle toe going out both ways the same time – he looked up and said, "It's worse than that. They don't bother to enslave endermen; they just kill them."

Emma and I gasped at the same time. "No!"

"They are killing endermen just for some stupid flowers and fruit?!?!" I yelled, totally outraged.

This time Mr. Blaze took over the story. "Yes, I'm afraid it is true. Clayton sends his allies from the Nether into the End where they kill any endermen who get in their way. The endermen are difficult to defeat though and Clayton is losing many forces. But, we've learned that Clayton is now working with an unknown person to spawn a massive army of zombie pigmen, ghasts, and blazes to send into the End for a massive battle."

I suddenly had a flash of Entity 303 in my mind. *Could that be who was working with Clayton?* I shook my head to clear the image. I needed to think clearly.

I could not believe what I was hearing. Emma and I had stumbled into the middle of a "battle of the century"-type scenario. This made my great great Gramps' killing of ten zombies look like playing tic-tac-toe. I couldn't believe how greedy Clayton was. He already controlled most of the resources of the Nether and was richer than anyone in the entire Overworld. In fact, his personal wealth was probably greater than half of the population of the Overworld. And now he wanted the End.

Savage.

"Is that why you are here in the Overworld?" Emma asked. "To prevent Clayton's invasion?"

The enderman nodded slowly. "Yes. We cannot wait for war to come to us. We are bringing war to Capitol City."

I couldn't believe that war was coming. I'd never seen a war. I had never been in a war. But, I had taken history class in school, and sort of paid attention. I knew war wasn't fun. I knew lots of people would vanish into puffs of smoke and respawn. Maybe their respawns would then become involved in the war and they might respawn multiple times before the war was over. It was horrible to think about.

Emma put her hands on her hips and looked directly at the enderman. "So you are just going to lead an enderman army to Capitol City and kill everybody? That's ridiculous. What kind of mob are you?"

The enderman stiffened. You could tell he was not used to anyone addressing him so impolitely. But he knew this was serious business and he knew that Emma was right to be upset in her own way. Or, if not right, at least it was understandable.

"We do not intend to start a war without an attempt at negotiations," said the enderman. "We will march our army to Capitol City and request the surrender of the entire Dretsky family. If they surrender, everything will end; if not, we go to war."

"The entire family?" I asked in shock. "Can't you just take Clayton and his greedy father away? You couldn't mean that Claire is involved in this, could you?"

Emma shot me a dirty look for bringing up Claire.

The enderman stared at me in the eyes. He blinked three times. Then, he turned around and, without a word, walked into the end portal.

'"What the heck was that?" I asked. The remaining endermen simply looked at me and shook their heads, before jumping into the end portal.

"Isn't anyone going to explain why he has to take the entire family?" I yelled.

Day 29 – Afternoon and Evening

After the three endermen disappeared, Mr. Blaze took us down a staircase that was hidden in the floor. He lifted up a rock and the staircase was there. We followed him down the stairs through some tunnels and up into the sub-basement of his bookshop.

"You two stay here while I go tend to my customers. There's some food in that cabinet over there, and you can take a nap in the one of those chairs," he said, pointing to what looked like the most uncomfortable chairs ever crafted in the history of Minecraft. "At the end of the day I'll come back down here and communicate with your parents to let them know you're both still alive."

"About that," asked Emma, "since Clayton knows we have escaped and were rescued by an enderman, what is the point in hiding?"

Mr. Blaze sighed. "The point is that if Clayton finds you, he will capture you and torture you until you tell him why the enderman was here. He's not stupid. He'll know it has something to do with his exploitation of the End."

"Torture? Would he really do that?" I asked, completely overwhelmed.

Mr. Blaze nodded silently. "So, stay here. I'll come back when I can."

* * *

In Mr. Blaze's absence, Emma and I sat around completely bored. You'd think that in a bookstore there would be all kinds of great stuff to read, but this basement didn't have any books in it. I guess because it was a secret hideout type of location Mr. Blaze didn't want to put any books in here and accidentally send one of his employees down here to get something and discover the place.

The boredom meant that I had nothing else to do except worry about my parents. I knew they had already been told by Biff's father that I was "dead," and there was nothing I could do. I knew that if Emma and I revealed our presence now, Clayton or his henchmen would find us, torture us, and then kill us and maybe our families.

He. Was. So. Evil.

Finally, after many hours and countless tears of frustration, despair, and rage, Mr. Blaze returned. He asked us how we were doing. We both complained about the boredom.

"Well, get ready, because this will be anything but boring," he said with a serious voice, but a twinkle in his eye.

Mr. Blaze told us to back away and remain silent while he placed the dream into the minds of our parents.

It was eerie.

Mr. Blaze began to move his arms in a strange, repeated pattern. Soon, bubbles materialized in front of him and then a foggy mist floated before his face. In the mist I could see my parents sleeping and Emma's parents sleeping. It made me sad. I saw that my parents' faces were streaked with tears, and my mom appeared to be crying in her sleep. I started crying too.

And then Mr. Blaze began to move his hands in another strange pattern and whisper words I couldn't quite understand, though I managed to catch a few of them: "don't worry" "alive" "home soon" "love you" "happiness".

As he made the strange motions and said these words I watched as my parents and Emma's parents appeared to smile in their sleep. My mom's eyes stopped gushing tears. They all sighed like they were very relaxed and then the foggy mist vanished.

Mr. Blaze, suddenly exhausted, sat down on a chair.

"That was astonishing, Mr. Blaze," said Emma, her voice cracking with emotion.

I nodded my head and wiped a few tears from my checks. "Yeah. It was ... hurrr ... super cool ... and ... hurrr ... amazing."

Emma looked at me like I was an idiot. Wordsmithing was never my strong suit. Plus, I was still emotional from seeing my parents and not being able to talk to them.

Mr. Blaze wiped beads of sweat from his forehead and said, "Thank you. That's really hard work. Much more difficult than possessing people. There's two-way communication between the subject of the suggestion, unlike possession which is a one-way street. And four people at once ... whew, it was exhausting. I had to hold four conversations at the same time. I should've only done one set of parents at the time."

"So, they know we're alive now?" I asked.

Mr. Blaze tilted his head from side to side. "Yes and no. They will have a certainty in their hearts that you are alive, but they will have no basis in fact for this belief. They will remain with the belief you are alive for at least a week, before the suggestion starts to wear off and they become distraught again. But that's plenty of time. The endermen should be back tomorrow and their ultimatum to Capitol City will likely happen very soon thereafter, well within a week's time."

I nodded and then said, "About that ultimatum. Why the entire Dretsky family? Claire seems okay, and even Clayton's mother didn't seem like she was very involved in the business."

Mr. Blaze considered my question for moment and then said, "Have you heard about the rainbow creeper religion?"

My blood turned to ice. Another reference to the rainbow creeper religion. "Yes," I said. "In fact, I was mentioning it to Emma a while ago."

"Well, then you probably know it's an ancient religion that broke away from the worship of Notch, the true creator of all Minecraft. Those who worship the rainbow creeper worship only power and wealth, at the expense of all else. We have reason to believe that Claire and her mother are members of the rainbow creeper religion," said Mr. Blaze solemnly.

"No, it can't be," I said. Then I remembered the robe with the rainbow creeper logo on it. Claire had said it was just a new fashion, but was it? Or was it a way to show others that she was a believer? And come to think of it, she'd worn that robe while we were in Creeper Junction, which Biff's father said was the place where the creeper worshipers had settled several hundred years ago. It was all starting to make sense, or, at least, it was all lining up to be a good conspiracy theory, if nothing else.

"So, are you saying that Clayton and his father are also adherents to the rainbow creeper religion?" asked Emma. "I mean, after all, they seem to be only interested in wealth and power as well."

Mr. Blaze nodded. "I assume that is the case. The worship of the Rainbow Creeper is normally passed down through families. It is rare for anyone to join the religion from the outside."

Emma stood quietly, lost in thought. She rolled her head around, stretching her neck. Then, she asked, "Are the endermen fighting against the Dretskys or are they fighting against the rainbow creeper religion?"

Mr. Blaze appeared surprised by this question, and, somewhat suspiciously, changed the subject. "Will you look at the time? It is late. You kids need to get to sleep, and so do I. See you tomorrow." And with that, Mr. Blaze ran up the stairs and left us alone.

I looked at Emma. "Why did he get so freaked out by your question?"

"That's what I'd like to find out."

Day 30 – Morning

At first light, Mr. Blaze came down the stairs, bringing with him a breakfast consisting of warm bread, carrots, and fried chicken. He also brought a few Minecraft diaries with him.

"I was rude yesterday in not bringing you any books. It looks like you may need to stay down here a few more hours, so I brought you some reading material in case you got bored," he said.

I saw that the books he had brought were books I read before but that I would be happy to read again. I grabbed a copy of the *Complete Baby Zeke: The Diary of a Chicken Jockey* while Emma pointed at one of the other books and said, "*Diary of a Spider Chicken*? What the heck's a spider chicken?"

Mr. Blaze shrugged. "I have no idea, but it is a pretty popular book in my store, so I thought I'd bring it down here."

Emma nodded her head. "Okay, hurrr. Maybe I'll read it."

Mr. Blaze explained that he was waiting for final word from the leader of the endermen that the attack was ready to go. Once he received word, he would come get us so that he could release us to our parents because there would no longer be any need to keep the secret of the pending enderman attack.

"Okay, sounds good," I said. Mr. Blaze smiled and then walked back up the stairs and shut the door.

Emma and I read our books quietly for about twenty minutes. But then Emma put her book down, stood up, and started pacing back and forth. I could tell something was wrong.

"What is it?"

She stopped pacing and looked at me. "We can't just let them declare war on Capitol City because Clayton's family is a bunch of greedy villagers. Think of all the innocent villagers who will die in such a confrontation!"

"I agree, but what can we do? The Ender Army is far more powerful than the Zombie Bane police force. Besides, the decision is really up to Clayton and his dad whether they are going to surrender."

Emma bit her fingernails nervously. "I wish I could think of something. It seems like there should be a way for the endermen to get satisfaction for the horrible things Clayton has done but without destroying an entire city."

"That's exactly what the enderman told us the other day. He was going to ask Clayton to surrender, and if he did, there would be no war."

Emma laughed sarcastically. "You and I both know that Clayton's insane. He will never surrender. He would gladly sacrifice thousands of villager lives if it would mean he could make more money."

I had to admit, she was probably right. Of course, once everyone found out how evil Clayton was, I'm not sure he would be able to live peacefully much longer. On the other hand, insane maniacs have a way of staying around and surviving things that you didn't think they could. This gave me a crazy idea.

"Why don't we ask Herobrine what to do?" I suggested, only half joking.

Emma's jaw fell open. "What are you talking about? Why would Herobrine want to give us any advice? And besides, how the heck would we get in contact with him in the first place?"

"I have no idea. It's just ... when I saw those visions of Herobrine and Entity 303, and I thought they were real, Herobrine said something to me about having to solve a puzzle." I shrugged. "I dunno. Maybe he can give us some advice."

"But didn't you tell me earlier that those visions of Herobrine and Entity 303 were only put in your head by Clayton's Evoker?"

"Yes ... I mean, that is what he *said*, anyway. But who knows when it comes to Herobrine. Maybe he piggybacked on the vision and actually was there. And, *what if* Herobrine would help us? I mean, he's an insane maniac, but he's also an attention hog and a narcissist. He doesn't want to have to share the world's attention with someone as powerful as Clayton. He wants to be the most powerful thing in the world, other than Notch."

There was a twinkle in Emma's eye. She seemed to be following my logic or illogic as the case may be. "Maybe Mr. Blaze will know how to get in contact with Herobrine? He seems to know a lot of rather surprising things."

I smiled. "Yeah. And, we can run our plan by him and maybe he'll agree that it could work."

Emma returned to her pacing and I returned to reading my book. In fact, I was at a scene where Baby Zeke confronts Herobrine and he ... well ... I don't want to give a spoiler, but it was pretty awesome.

Maybe I could get to meet Herobrine like Baby Zeke did and people would want to read my diary. I don't know, maybe I'm just being stupid. I've been keeping this diary for a while and I don't know if I'll ever publish it. But if I did, I suppose some people might be interested in the story.

* * *

Another couple of hours passed before Mr. Blaze finally came down the stairs and said, "The endermen are ready. You can leave and go home to your parents now."

"Actually, we'd like to stay for a bit," said Emma.

Mr. Blaze was shocked. "Don't you want to go home to your parents and prove to them that you're alive?"

"Of course," said Emma. "But you've given them the suggestion vision and now they know we're alive so it could wait a little bit." Emma paused and then said, "We might have a way to avoid this war between the endermen and Capitol City."

Mr. Blaze squinted his eyes and then leaned back against the wall crossing his arms in front of him. "Really? You know of a way to get Clayton to surrender? Because that's the only way the endermen won't attack."

"Not yet, but we think we know someone who could help," I said.

Mr. Blaze looked at me and rubbed his chin. He smiled that condescending smile that adults use when they know a kid is going to say something lame, but want to appear like they are listening. "Who would that be?"

"Herobrine," Emma and I said in unison.

Mr. Blaze uncrossed his arms and slapped both of his cheeks with his hands and opened his mouth in the shape of an O. Obviously, he was shocked. "I'm shocked!" he said. (*Called it!*) "How do you think Herobrine can help?"

"Well, it was Jimmy's idea," said Emma. "But, we think Herobrine wants to remain the most dominant force in the world, other than Notch. I'm sure he does not like Clayton. So, maybe he could come up with a way to take away Clayton's power but without the risk of the endermen killing half the population of Capitol City."

Mr. Blaze nodded his head up and down. "I suppose your idea makes some sense, but why wouldn't Herobrine just want the endermen to destroy all of Capitol City? What does Herobrine care about the villagers who live there?"

"Herobrine's obviously evil, no doubt," I said. "But, I don't think he's *that* evil. After all, the only way to be powerful is to have people *know* that you're powerful. That's why Clayton wants to be rich, so people know that he's rich. If he lived in the Overworld all by himself, there would be no point to amassing such a huge fortune."

Mr. Blaze raised his eyebrows and pursed his lips and then nodded his head, agreeing with me. "That's a very astute observation. So, basically, what you're saying is that Herobrine is going to help us defeat Clayton because Clayton's taking away the power he feels because people are beginning to fear Clayton more than they fear Herobrine, right?"

I shrugged. "I guess so. Makes sense."

"Yes, that's exactly what Jimmy is saying," said Emma. "At least, it's worth a try. Herobrine's pretty devious, so he might be able to come up with something that would avoid war entirely while still stopping Clayton."

"I've got to hand it to you kids, that's a pretty interesting idea. I just wish I knew how to contact Herobrine," said Mr. Blaze.

I was crestfallen. I had assumed Mr. Blaze with all his books about the occult and about magic would have some idea about how to contact the white-eyed freak. "Really? You don't know?"

Mr. Blaze shook his head. "I wish I could, but I don't think anyone knows how to do that."

At that moment the leader of the endermen materialized in the room in which we were talking. He stood there, hunched slightly so that his head wouldn't hit the low ceiling.

He looked at all three of us and then in particular at me, his rectangular purple eyes boring into my soul. I could see the future and the past. I was resurrected and killed and reborn again. I learned 1000 languages and forgot 5000 more. His eyes were like the depths of eternity.

And then he said, "I know how to contact Herobrine."

Day 30 – Afternoon

After dropping his knowledge bomb on us about Herobrine, the enderman refused to tell us how to contact him! Instead, he demanded that we gather our things and teleport with him to the cavern where the Ender Army had gathered.

I whined and cried like a baby. I stomped my feet on the ground and hit my head against the wall, demanding that he tell me how to contact Herobrine, but he steadfastly refused. "I will tell you later," was all he said.

Emma was much more mature than I was, but she was upset as well. She threatened to leave and go back to her parents' house and abandon the whole plan, but the enderman calmed her by telling her that our idea was a good one and that she needed to help.

So, the mystery hung in the air and we wondered what was going to happen.

When we teleported to the Ender Army assembly site, there were thousands of endermen inside a massive cavern. They were bouncing around and teleporting here and there and everywhere. They were on edge. They were ready to attack.

But, when they saw we had arrived, they became suddenly still and silent before they each got down on one knee.

"What the heck is that all about?" I asked, looking at our enderman companion. "It's like they think you're famous or something." I started laughing at the ridiculousness of my suggestion ... until I realized no one else was laughing.

"Jimmy," hissed Mr. Blaze out the side of his mouth, "he *is* the Ender King!"

Mooshroom flops, I thought.

I turned and looked at the enderman who I had just thought was some high-ranking officer in the Ender Army, not the Ender King himself! He had seemed to double in size since we had arrived. His looked down at me with his flat purple eyes regarding me.

"How's the weather up there?" I said, hoping to lighten the mood with my feeble attempt at humor.

The endermen in the room gasped and began to move toward me. The Ender King held out a hand commanding them to stop.

Would they have killed me for disrespecting their king?

I pulled at my collar to let out some of the heat I was now feeling. "So, it's true then?" I managed to squeak.

"Yes, I am the Ender King," he said. His voice seemed to have grown deeper as well, more regal.

"So, do you still want to help us contact the H man, or do you have more important things to do?" I asked.

Rather than answering my question, the Ender King pointed to a small alcove in the cavern. "You children wait in the alcove. I must speak with Mr. Blaze. Alone."

I can tell you, if you ever come face-to-face with an enderman, especially the Ender King, you'll do what he says. Emma and I walked over to the alcove and sat down.

"This is so stupid," I said. "I know he's the King and all, but why doesn't he just tell us how to contact Herobrine. So selfish." I crossed my arms and pouted.

Emma shrugged. "Probably because he doesn't really know how. He probably just wants us around so that he can use this as a bargaining chip with Clayton."

I gasped. "You don't think he would sacrifice us to get what he wants from Clayton?" Beads of sweat began to pour out of my forehead. My normally stylish blonde hair became wet and stringy. My armpits were getting sweaty. I could feel the world closing in. I was going to pass out.

"Of course not," said Emma. "He probably just wants us as witnesses. Maybe he wants us to tell the other villagers in Capitol City what we've seen. Help convince them to turn over the evil Dretskys."

"That's a pretty good idea you have. That probably is what he wants us to do," I said, trying to reassure myself that I wasn't about to meet my end.

At that moment the Ender King and Mr. Blaze came over.

"Okay, kids, let's go contact Herobrine," said Mr. Blaze.

"So, you do know how to contact Herobrine?" I asked, looking at the Ender King.

The Ender King shook his head at me, expressing his disappointment. "Of course. I never lie."

"Jimmy, you need to keep your mouth shut for a while. Do you want the King's help or not?" asked Mr. Blaze.

"Yes, of course. Sorry."

The Ender King told the three of us to stand next to each other. Once we were shoulder to shoulder, the Ender King wrapped his arms around us and everything vanished.

* * *

An instant later, we were on top of a mountain in the extreme hills biome. Before us was nothing but trees. I turned around and could see some llamas grazing on grass in the valley below.

I looked to the Ender King and said, "We're meeting Herobrine in a forest?"

"Not exactly. Follow me," said the Ender King as he walked forward into the trees.

We walked through the trees for less than a minute when the Ender King reached out his hand and knocked on what appeared to be thin air as if it were door. I stared in awe as the air suddenly shimmered and was replaced by the walls of an obsidian structure. Even the door, which I could now plainly see, was made of obsidian.

"Whoa," I said. "I bet this is a strong fortress."

Emma was amazed too. "This is where Herobrine lives?"

"He lives here for the time being," said the Ender King with a hint of mystery.

At that moment the door cracked open. My knees began to tremble. I was about to come face-to-face with the greatest menace Minecraft had ever known, that white eyed freak, Herobrine. I was starting to take shallow, rapid breaths, my fight-or-flight reflex activating in anticipation of what I was about to see.

The door opened slightly more.

I began to mumble aloud, "Oh, my Notch! Oh, my Notch! Oh, my Notch!" hoping that invoking the name of the Great Creator would protect me from what was to come.

Emma hit me on the arm with the back of her hand. "Jimmy, get a hold of yourself."

"Yeah," said Mr. Blaze. "Just relax."

But I couldn't relax. I couldn't believe this was about to happen. I'd seen Herobrine in the mirror, but I didn't even know if that had been the real Herobrine or just some cruel trick. Now, I was about to see him for real. I was about to lose it.

When the door opened all the way, I screamed! Standing before me in the doorway was ... hurrr ... oh, how embarrassing, now I can't believe that I screamed. It was a small chicken.

"How may help you?" asked the chicken.

The Ender King spoke. "Chicken. We desire an audience with Herobrine."

The chicken craned his neck back almost on a 90° angle in order to be able to look at the Ender King's face. "And whom shall I say is calling?"

"You can tell him it's the Ender King and his friends."

Now, it was the chicken's turn to scream. He let out a high-pitched cluck, which, I suppose, was equivalent to a scream. Or maybe how they gasped or something like that. I didn't have much experience with chickens, except for eating them. But the chicken doorman was clearly impressed. He backed away from the door in a bowed position and lifted his left wing to indicate that we should enter.

The Ender King entered first followed by Mr. Blaze and then Emma. I followed last, not to be polite, but because I was so scared that I didn't want to go into the building. (Yeah, this is another one of those instances where I almost peed my robe.)

The chicken led us to a small room with chairs and a few books in it. He said, "Please make yourselves comfortable. I will go inform master Herobrine that you have arrived."

The Ender King looked at the chicken and said, "Please hurry. We don't have much time." The chicken saluted the King with his right wing and then scurried away to find his master.

I sat down on a chair and looked over at the Ender King. "How did you know Herobrine lived here?"

The Ender King shrugged his long skinny black shoulders. "I always know where Herobrine is."

"How do you know that?" I asked.

The Ender King looked at me with those freakish purple rectangular eyes of his and said, "I won't tell you." And just like that, the subject was closed. Whatever. I didn't have to know every single secret of Minecraft. I wasn't like Clayton.

Emma was looking around the room and flipping through the books. They were all written in a strange language that she didn't understand. It consisted of numbers and letters and even some pictures mixed in for good measure. She took one of the books and showed it to Mr. Blaze. "Do you know what language this is?"

Mr. Blaze took the book and studied it. "I believe it's called hexadecimal hieroglyphics. It is said that Herobrine invented his own language when he first manifested as a glitch and then used it to write diaries. Since no one else can read it, he probably just left these books out. I bet they are his personal diaries." Mr. Blaze handed the book back to Emma.

When she took the book back, her hands were shaking slightly. "Wow. I wish I could read this. I bet it would be fascinating." Emma put the book down and sat in a chair to wait for Herobrine to arrive.

We didn't have to wait long. A few moments later the chicken returned with a second chicken. Together they clucked a little song and then announced, "King, lady, and gentlemen, the great and majestic Herobrine arrives." As they finished their statement they both bowed and raised their wings in praise.

We all looked down to the end of the hall. And, there he was, in the flesh, Herobrine.

Herobrine stood there with his arms outstretched, as if waiting for us to applaud his presence. Of course we did not. Emma and I were too shocked to do anything. Mr. Blaze seemed calm, but still in awe of being in Herobrine's presence. Only the Ender King seemed bored.

Herobrine walked toward us and when he got close enough, he said, "Endy! What up, my royal highness?"

The King shook his head. "Why are you always trying to be dope?"

Herobrine laughed. "I'm not *trying* to *be* dope, I *am* dope."

The King shook his head again. "Okay, let's stop pandering to the kids in the room, who don't use the term 'dope' anyway since it is totally outdated, and instead, let's get down to business. We're here to talk about Clayton Dretsky."

At the mention of Clayton's name, Herobrine's face turned a dark, angry red. He clenched his fists and said, "What do you want to talk about?"

The Ender King looked at Emma and me and said, "This is your idea kids, you tell him."

I couldn't believe it. Here I was face to face with Herobrine. I tried to talk but my lips wouldn't move. My mouth went dry. My brain stopped working. I. Was. Frozen.

Thankfully, Emma was a little braver than I. She spoke right up. "Herobrine, we were hoping you could give us some ideas."

Herobrine raised an eyebrow curiously. "Ideas? For what? Are you thinking about blowing something up?" said Herobrine with an evil chuckle as he rubbed his hands together gleefully.

"No, I am not," said Emma. "But, the Ender King is."

"Can I watch? Can I watch?" said Herobrine like a little kid.

"No, you may not," said the Ender King.

Herobrine pouted and slumped his shoulders. "You just try to stop me."

Emma rolled her eyes. "Can you please chill? Look, the Ender King wants to stop Clayton Dretsky from killing his people. He's resigned himself to war with the Dretskys and all of Capitol City, if necessary. But, Jimmy and I were thinking that you might be able to come up with some way to defeat the Dretskys without full-blown war."

Herobrine took a deep breath and said, "I hate to admit this, but the Dretskys are very powerful. If they were just a normal villager family, I could just put some TNT in their house or curse them with some sort of inability to make money, but they have too much protection: Evokers, Vindicators, Illusioners, allied mobs, and all manner of spells and potions."

I finally regained my ability to speak. "Are you saying there's no way to defeat them except through war?"

Herobrine shot me an angry look. "I didn't say that. I just said it would be difficult. It might take some ... creativity."

"So what you got?" I asked.

This time, Herobrine didn't just shoot me an angry look. In addition, he suddenly quadrupled in size so he was almost as tall as the Ender King. He then looked down upon me and pointed his big fat finger at my face and said, "Be quiet you pathetic worm."

So this was totally a pee-my-robe moment; the worst ever. The fact that I didn't pee my robe then and there proved to me that there was probably nothing in the entire world that could ever make me pee my robe. On the one hand, I was proud of not peeing myself; on the other hand, there was a gigantic Herobrine standing in front of me.

"I'm sorry," I squeaked.

Herobrine shrunk down to his more typical size and said, "Let me think about your request. I'll come up with something. Where can I find you in about three hours?"

"We will be blockading Capitol City by then," said the Ender King. "I will give you four hours. If you do not return with a good idea, then my army will march on Capitol City."

Day 30 - Two hours later

After we finished talking to Herobrine, the Ender King teleported us back to the assembly chamber where his army awaited.

Emma and I had a snack consisting of a pork chop, an apple, a few watermelon slices, and water. Mr. Blaze went with the Ender King to meet with the Army generals in order to make final preparations for the assault on Capitol City

* * *

About two hours after we had left Herobrine's fortress, the Ender King approached us and told us that it was time. We followed the Ender King back to the main area of the chamber. We watched as the Ender King climbed to the top of a dais and addressed his troops.

"The Dretskys came into our realm to steal end stone and chorus flowers. They killed our people so they could open florist shops selling chorus flowers and fruit stands selling chorus fruit!"

The assembled army booed and hissed. They teleported in chaotic fashion showing their disapproval. It looked like a rapidly spreading ink stain.

The Ender King continued. "The lives of endermen are worth far more than end stone and chorus flowers! But the lives of the Dretskys and anyone who supports them aren't even worth a speck of cobblestone."

The army roared with approval!

"And so, my great army, we go to Capitol City to issue an ultimatum. But we must be prepared for it to be refused. And we must be prepared to take on the ultimate burden and to bear the ultimate sacrifice. For our people! For our realm!" The Ender King raised his fist to the air to punctuate his final statement.

The army erupted into the most chaotically loud, deafening cheer I had ever heard. It was so loud that I *felt* it more than I *heard* it. The vibrations of the cheering passed through my body and shook my brain, they were so strong. I had to hold onto the wall to keep from falling down. In short, I was shook.

The Ender King raised his hands, imploring the crowd for silence. "I will teleport first. Once I have left, I want all of you to teleport at the same time to my coordinates."

The Ender King turned around and walked over to Emma, Mr. Blaze, and me. He looked at us and said, "Ready?"

We all nodded our heads. The Ender King embraced us with his long arms and the room vanished.

The next thing we knew we were standing about 200 yards from the front gate of Capitol City. Less than one second later, several thousand endermen teleported to our location and stood arrayed behind us.

The Ender King then commanded, "Encircle the city!"

And with that the thousands of endermen dispersed, teleporting to different locations in order to form a ring around the city, completely blocking it off from the outside world.

There were several guards standing on the guard towers of Capitol City. You could see the shock on their faces even from the distance where we stood. One of them shouted, "What do you otherworldly freaks want?"

The Ender King quickly teleported to within a few feet of the guard slapped him across the face and then teleported back. "Bring us the mayor!" he shouted. "We have demands."

The guard, his slapped face turning bright red, shouted, "Okay ... hurrr ... I'll be right back."

We waited in silence for about five minutes until the guard returned and yelled, "Here comes the mayor!"

We watched as a man slowly made his way up the stairs. When he came into view, I gasped. It was Clayton's father, Mr. Dretsky!

"I am the mayor," he shouted. "What is it that you wish to discuss?"

"I am the Ender King. Clayton Dretsky, who I believe is your son, has been sending people into the End to steal our resources. He has been killing my people. It must stop immediately or we will destroy Capitol City."

Mr. Dretsky pretended like he had no idea what the Ender King was talking about. "I daresay you are mistaken, sir. My son would do nothing of the kind. He's too busy with his studies."

The Ender King laughed. "Stop lying. I have seen my people struck down in person. I know it is your son, Clayton, and his henchmen who do it. You have one hour to present Clayton, along with the rest of your family, for arrest and punishment. If you do not, we will attack the city."

The mayor said nothing more but walked away.

I tapped Mr. Blaze on the shoulder and whispered, "Do you think they will surrender? I'd be pretty scared if I saw an army of endermen surrounding my town."

Mr. Blaze shrugged. "Any other village would surrender immediately. But, you heard what Herobrine said about all the magical and strange powers the Dretskys have at their disposal. They might be just crazy enough to fight the Ender Army, and they might be able win."

I was shocked. I couldn't believe the Dretsky family could be so powerful. Were all billionaires this powerful? Actually, were there any other billionaires in the Overworld?

After that, we waited. There was no chitchat, no goofing around, no playing games. This was it. The ultimatum had been issued. Unless Herobrine showed up with an amazing idea, it would either be surrender or war.

* * *

I wasn't sure how the Ender King was keeping track of the passing of one hour, there were no clocks in sight, but somehow he knew. After one hour had passed, he yelled, "Guard! Bring Clayton and the Dretsky family to me now, or else!"

The guard replied nervously, "Just a second Mr. ... hurrr ... Mr. King, sir. Let me see what the mayor has decided."

Less than a minute later the mayor, Clayton Dretsky's father, and Clayton appeared on the guard tower. Someone else was there with them. It was hard to see but ....

"Is that Claire?!?" said Emma.

She was right! Did that mean Claire was as evil as her brother? Had she been lying to me all along? Was she part of the rainbow creeper religion?

Mr. Dretsky took a deep breath and shouted, "The answer is no!"

The Ender King sighed and bowed his head for a few seconds but then when he raised it, his face was resolute. "In that case, prepare to meet your end."

The Ender King suddenly swelled to ten times his normally massive size. He was as tall as all but a handful of buildings in Capitol City. He took a deep breath and was about to yell an order to his troops when suddenly Herobrine appeared floating in the sky in between the Ender King and Capitol City.

"Wait! I, the great Herobrine, have a better idea!"

Last minute appearance? Total drama queen!

I shouted, "Yeah, Herobrine! H gonna give it to ya! Gonna give it to ya! Yeah, H gonna give it to ya! First we gonna rock, then we gonna roll!"

Everyone looked at me like I was a complete idiot. They didn't understand that the only reason Herobrine was here was because of the great idea that Emma and I had to ask him to come up with something other than war to settle this problem. And now he was here. I could not wait to hear his idea.

The Ender King looked at Herobrine floating in the sky and said, "What is it? This better be good."

Herobrine smiled with glee as he said, "Rather than by war, we will solve this dispute by having a surf contest."

I couldn't believe what I was hearing. It was amazing. I raised my fist into the air and shouted, "Yeah, Herobrine! Great idea, H-man!" I then proceeded to hoot and holler and express my great joy at the idea which Herobrine had brought to us in order to avert war.

But not everyone shared my enthusiasm. In fact, no one else did.

As I was still shaking my fist in the air and hooting and hollering and jumping up and down, the Ender King stretched out his long black arm, placed it on top of my head, and pressed down firmly so that I could jump no more.

I looked over at him and said, "What's wrong, King? This is a great idea."

Herobrine continued to hover in the air smiling smugly at his own awesomeness.

The Ender King looked at Herobrine and said, "That is the stupidest idea I have ever heard in my entire life! You have done nothing to avert war. Why did we even bother asking you for help?!?"

The situation suddenly felt ominous. This was it. Looking into the flat purple eyes of the Ender King, I could see he was about to give the order to attack Capitol City. I looked across the open plain between where we stood and where Clayton and his father and Claire stood. I felt an impending sense of dread.

I watched the Ender King raise his arm and press his fist into the air as high as he could. I saw him take a deep breath. I saw him open his mouth. I was expecting to hear him yell something like, "Charge!" or maybe "Attack!" or even something as mundane as "Go get 'em, boys!"

But none of that happened

Instead there was a blinding flash of light, so bright that I thought I would be rendered sightless, my retinas seared. Everyone present, even the Ender King and Herobrine gasped at the sight of the light. In fact, Herobrine plunged to the earth, but like a cat, landed on his feet.

The blinding light continued for a few seconds such that we all had to shield our eyes from it.

The light's intensity began to decrease slowly. As I regained my vision I started to look around for the source of the light. I didn't know anything could be so bright without also emitting heat. But there had been no fire and no explosion, only an instantaneous brightness.

I looked to my left and saw Herobrine on the ground looking up with concern. I glanced to my right and saw the Ender King also looking up, expressionless. I swiveled my head back and forth and noticed that others were looking up as well. Since everyone was doing it, I thought I might as well do it too.

I looked up.

And, behold! There, floating above everyone, was Notch himself!!!

I quickly felt my knees trembling with fear and awe. The Creator of all the world was floating above us. Floating above what had almost become a battlefield for an epic battle. But now, it had become a holy place. A place where villagers would remember for generations that Notch had manifested his divine presence.

But why? Why had he appeared now? It made no sense. Fortunately, Notch explained.

"My creations," he began with a deep intonation. "I do not approve of your plans for war. The endermen deserve respect and Capitol City deserves to survive."

To my astonishment, the Ender King stood up and then addressed Notch rather crossly, "Of course, we deserve respect! But there must be payment for the horrible crimes visited upon the endermen by the Dretsky family!"

Notch nodded his head slightly and blinked his eyes twice. "I will prevent the Dretsky family or their minions from ever returning to the End. Is that not enough to satisfy you?"

The Ender King laughed. "No. But it's a start. I will be satisfied only when the Dretsky family faces the ultimate humiliation. Especially, that terrible Clayton Dretsky."

I heard a smaller voice from far away shout, "I resent that! You can't talk ... hurrr ... to me like that!"

It was Clayton yelling from the top of the wall surrounding Capitol City.

Notch looked over at Clayton and said, "Clayton, you have been behaving badly towards the endermen. You have also been behaving badly by enslaving innocent villagers. I have just now freed them with my magical powers. I also teleported them back to their homes where they can be with their loved ones once more."

Clayton screamed like a little 3-year-old baby. "You can't do that to me, Notch! I've worked too hard to create my businesses to have you take them away at your whim."

Notch suddenly swelled in size. He was easily one hundred times larger than he had been only a second ago. I trembled at the sight. Not in my wildest dreams or nightmares had I ever thought I would see something like this!

Notch hovered above all of us and blotted out the sun. He pointed a gigantic finger directly at Clayton and said, "You know nothing of creating. I created the entire world of Minecraft, not some ridiculous, meaningless multi-billion dollar business! Without me, you wouldn't even exist. Show some respect."

If Notch had been saying those things to me in his gigantic form, I guarantee I would've peed in my robe. Who's to say Clayton didn't? But from where I stood, I couldn't get a clear look.

At this point Clayton's father intervened and stepped in front of Clayton. "Oh, great Notch. My son is sorry for what he did and will not do it again. Besides, he has other business ventures which do not require him to ... hurrr ... requisition ... hurrr ... labor in the manner in which he has previously."

Notch shrank back to his normal size and, addressing Mr. Dretsky, said, "I suppose one of these other businesses to which you refer is the wave pool?"

Mr. Dretsky nodded his head.

Notch then looked over in the direction of Emma and me and said, "Jimmy Slade and Emma Watson. You two also have created a surf park, right?"

"Yes, sir, we did," said Emma.

"Yeah, and we did it first! Clayton stole our idea!" I said.

"Did not," yelled Clayton from across the plain.

"Did too," I retorted.

"Did not," responded Clayton.

"Did –"

"ENOUGH!" bellowed Notch. Notch hovered above everyone for a few seconds in silence, like an elderly substitute teacher after breaking up a spitwad fight between students in her classroom. Everyone felt shame in his presence.

No one else would speak. By the expression on Notch's face, it appeared as though he were thinking about something, planning something in his mysterious, amazing mind which had created everything I could see in front of me, except, of course, Notch himself. Notch had been created from the formless vastness of space, by who or what, no one knew.

Notch tapped his finger against his lips, continuing to think. And then he said, "Herobrine was right."

"I was?" said Herobrine, taken by surprise. "I mean, I was! Yes, I rule!" he said, pumping his fist into the air.

Notch looked at Herobrine as if Herobrine were an annoying little baby with a bright green booger dangling from his nose. "Calm down, Herobrine. You know that I rule, not you."

Herobrine rolled his eyes and shook his head, but wisely stayed silent.

Notch then addressed everyone at once. "I think we *should* have a surf contest. The winner will get bragging rights for all of eternity as the winner of the first surfing contest in the history of Minecraft."

I couldn't believe this. There was actually going to be a surf contest like in the surf magazine I'd been given by that player so long ago. This was amazing.

Notch continued. "I am considering creating additional mobs and behaviors in what I am calling the

Update Aquatic to my creation. I've considered creating some new animals, such as dolphins and turtles, and new plants, such as seagrass and kelp. I'm also going to create underground structures and allow players and others to swim in the water better than they do currently. I also am considering adding ocean waves, and I want to see what this 'surfing' is all about."

I couldn't believe Notch was revealing his creation plans to us before they had even happened! And, he might be adding real waves to the oceans of the Overworld?!?! The Update Aquatic sounded awesome, but what the heck is a dolphin?

Notch continued. "We will hold the surf contest in three parts in three locations. The first contest will be held in the Dretsky wave pool in Capitol City. The second contest will be held at the Surf 'n Snack in Zombie Bane. The third and final contest will be held at a location to be disclosed later. The surf contest will involve teams. There will be a Capitol City team and there will be an End team. The captain of the Capitol City team is Clayton Dretsky. The captain of the End team is the Ender King. Each captain must select three teammates, for a total of four beings on a team. Those teammates will then have one week to practice for the first surf contest at the Dretsky wave pool."

The Ender King shook his head. "Notch, this is ridiculous. I refuse to participate in this farce."

Notch smiled at the Ender King. "You have no choice, old friend, for I am Notch and I have spoken.

The team winning two of the three contests will be declared the overall winner and will get to make fun of the loser of the surf contest for all of eternity. If you want to humiliate Clayton Dretsky, win the surf contest. I will not allow you to fight a war against Capitol City and kill thousands of innocent villagers when I have already forbidden anyone in the Dretsky family from traveling to the End. I have spoken."

And with that, Notch disappeared.

I have to say, I was surprised that Notch was condoning making fun of other people. On the other hand, he did stop a massive war in which thousands of villagers would have died. It was the lesser of two evils, I suppose.

I looked over at the Ender King and said, "Pick me! Pick me! I'm a good surfer. Put me on your team!"

I could tell the Ender King was annoyed by me, but much more annoyed by Notch. The King looked at me and said, "Fine. You're on the team. Who else should we have on the team?"

I thought about that. "Well, we could get my friend Laird on the team. He is a player from beyond Minecraft, but Notch didn't put any limits on who could be on the team. Laird's a really good surfer."

The Ender King sighed. "Okay, we'll get him too. We still need one more person."

I thought and thought. I didn't know anyone else other than Clayton Dretsky who was very good at surfing. We did have a week to practice though, so we needed someone with natural ability who could learn how to rip in a short time. I looked over at Emma. She had an expectant look on her face. I leaned over to the Ender King and said, "What about Emma? She knows how to surf already, and with practice, she could be pretty good."

The Ender King shrugged. He was being surprisingly chill about this whole process, considering the stakes. "Fine, she's on the team. That makes four."

I stood there, not quite sure what to do and then asked, "So ... hurrr ... should we head back to Zombie Bane so we can get our surfboards and then return to practice in the Capitol City wave pool?"

The Ender King looked at me. "One of my lieutenants will teleport you and Emma back to Zombie Bane. I need to return to the End for a day with my troops to regroup. I'll see you in Zombie Bane tomorrow, and then we can begin our practice for this asinine surf contest."

And with that, the Ender King and his entire army, except for one lieutenant, disappeared.

The remaining lieutenant walked over to Emma and I and wordlessly wrapped his arms around us. Just before we teleported, I could hear Clayton's maniacal laughter carrying across the plain.

END of Book 5

A Note from Dr. Block

I hope you liked this collection of the first five books in the *Surfer Villager* series. If you have a spare minute, would you mind leaving a review on your favorite online bookstore or review site?

And, don't forget to head over to my website – *DrBlockBooks.com* – and grab your **free copy** of my *Minecraft coloring and activity book*. Also, you can sign up for my email list to hear about new books when they come out. Or, if you prefer, follow my **Instagram** (*@drblockbooks*) or **Facebook** (*@drblockbooks*).

Thanks a million!

Dr. Block

Be sure to pick up your copy of *Diary of a Surfer Villager, Books 6-10*, to find out what happens next!

Be sure to check out my other books, including:

‍mation can be obtained
‍esting.com
‍‍e USA
‍236190420
‍V00002B/451

9 781733 695923